SINISTER WINDS

WRITTEN BY SHERRY A. BURTON

Sinister Winds ©2024
by Sherry A. Burton
Published by Dorry Press
Edited and Formatted by BZHercules.com
Cover by Laura J. Prevost
www.laurajprevostbookcovers.myportfolio.com

All rights reserved. No part of this book may be reproduced in any form or by any electronic or mechanical means, including information storage and retrieval systems—except in the case of brief quotations embodied in critical articles or reviews—without permission in writing from the author at sherryaburton@outlook.com This book is a work of fiction. The characters, events, and places portrayed in this book are products of the author's imagination and are either fictitious or are used fictitiously. Any similarity to real persons, living or dead, is purely coincidental and not intended by the author.

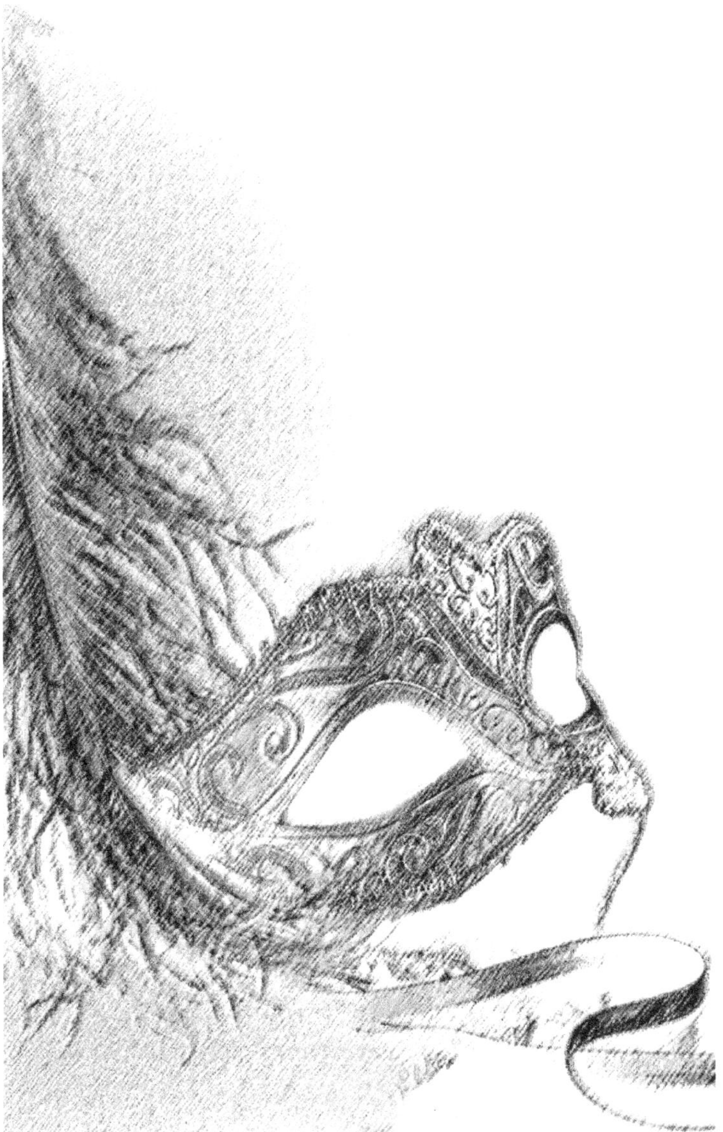

ALSO BY SHERRY A. BURTON

The Orphan Train Saga
Discovery (book one)
Shameless (book two)
Treachery (book three)
Guardian (book four)
Loyal (book five)
Patience (book six)
Endurance (book seven)

Orphan Train Extras
Ezra's Story

Jerry McNeal Series (Also in Audio)
Always Faithful (book one)
Ghostly Guidance (book two)
Rambling Spirit (book three)
Chosen Path (book four)
Port Hope (book five)
Cold Case (book six)
Wicked Winds (book seven)
Mystic Angel (book eight)
Uncanny Coincidence (book nine)
Chesapeake Chaos (book ten)
Village Shenanigans (book eleven)
Special Delivery (book twelve)
Spirit of Deadwood (a full-length Jerry McNeal novel, book thirteen)
Star Treatment (book fourteen)
Merry Me (book fifteen)

**Clean and Cozy Jerry McNeal Series Collection
(Compilations of the standalone Jerry McNeal series)**
The Jerry McNeal Clean and Cozy Edition Volume one
(books 1-3)
The Jerry McNeal Clean and Cozy Edition Volume two
(books 4-6)
The Jerry McNeal Clean and Cozy Edition Volume three
(books 7-9)
The Jerry McNeal Clean and Cozy Edition Volume four
(books 10-12)
The Jerry McNeal Clean and Cozy Edition Volume five
(books 13-15)

Romance Books *(*not clean* - sex and language)*
Tears of Betrayal
Love in the Bluegrass
Somewhere In My Dreams
The King of My Heart

Romance Books *(clean)*
Seems Like Yesterday

"Whispers of the Past" (a short story)

**Psychological Thrillers
Storm Series**
Surviving the Storm (book one, contains sex, language, and violence)
Sinister Winds (book two, contains language and violence)

A SPECIAL THANKS TO:

My editor, Beth, for allowing me to keep my voice.

My cover artist and media design guru, Laura Prevost, thanks for keeping me current.

My proofreader, Latisha Rich, for that extra set of eyes.

To my amazing team of beta readers, thank you for helping take a final look.

To my husband, thank you for your endless hours of researching, your help with all things genealogy, and for allowing me to bounce story ideas off of you.

CHAPTER ONE

Safe within the confines of the rescue helicopter, Abby glanced at the other evacuees and wondered if they knew she was a murderer. She forced her guilt aside as she watched Petty Officer Gomez, the Coast Guardsman who'd rescued her from the roof of her house, stand in the open doorway searching for more flood victims. Wearing a bright yellow helmet and orange flight suit with patches on the front and sleeves that went well with his dark brown skin, Gomez turned to the freckle-skinned man beside him and spoke into his mouthpiece as he extended his arm and pointed at something she could not see. The other man, who wore a white helmet and was dressed in an olive-green jumpsuit with a name patch that read "Kennedy," moved up beside him, holding tight to a safety line secured to the roof of the chopper. Gomez tapped the man's shoulder and pointed once more. Kennedy nodded and mouthed something Abby was unable to hear over the noise within the iron bird.

Kennedy moved aside, tapped the headset, and spoke once more. He must have been speaking to the pilot as the helicopter dipped and made a wide turn. A moment later, the helo stilled, and Kennedy clapped Gomez on the shoulder.

In a scenario that had repeated itself many times since her rescue, Gomez, who was holding on to a strap on the opposite side of the opening, lifted his hand to the guide wire, wrapped his right leg around it, and stepped out of the aircraft. He gave a nod to Kennedy, who reached for a lever to lower him. Kennedy took Gomez's place in the doorway, bracing himself as he looked after the man. Abby closed her eyes, only to be startled awake when Gomez returned with another victim. Kennedy worked to pry the woman's hands from Gomez's waist. As she watched Gomez lower once more, she wondered if the scenario was actually taking place or if she was in a nightmare that kept replaying over and over. Only it couldn't be a dream, as each time Gomez returned, he carried with him someone new. People who, like herself, had found themselves stranded on a steaming rooftop, praying for a miracle to save them.

Abby watched the opening with rapt attention, praying for the safety of whoever was out there along with the man who'd gone after them seemingly without fear.

Petty Officer Gomez might not have counted himself a miracle worker for doing the job he'd been trained to do, but to Abby and the six other passengers who had been rescued from the roof in the span of a scant few moments, the man—who looked like he was barely old enough to be out of high school—was an angel sent to them from the heavens. And each time he returned to the chopper and released his catch, those inside whispered thanks to the heavens above. Not that there was any need to whisper, as it was too loud to think, much less be heard over the roar of the helo.

Gomez wasn't looking for approval, as within seconds

of unhooking the person he'd just hoisted up, he stepped back into the opening, searching for his next conquest.

As Abby sat braced against the hard steel, watching him, she recalled her own rescue moments earlier. She'd fought him. She was sorry for that. But at the time, she thought it was her husband, Jacob, and wasn't about to allow the man to do the vile things he'd threatened before succumbing to his watery grave. She recalled Gomez's face when his words finally cut through the fog surrounding her brain and the look of concern as he clutched her up next to him and asked if anyone else was in the house. "My husband," she'd said, not wishing to speak the man's name for fear Jacob would somehow materialize and pull her into the watery grave with him.

Gomez looked at the foul-smelling water that surrounded the roof, his eyes telling her what she already knew. Jacob was indeed dead. He'd then secured her in the harness that fit under her arms and passed the strap between her legs before signaling the helicopter hovering overhead to pull them up. She felt a moment of panic when her feet left the roof, then another as her rescuer wrapped his arms around her, staring into her eyes, his boyish voice cracking as he told her she was safe, and he wasn't going to let anyone hurt her.

It was an odd statement, as if somehow he knew the hell she'd just endured, and one that had sent a chill racing up her spine even though it was much too hot for her to be cold. She'd lowered her eyes so he couldn't see the truth—that she was happy her husband was dead.

The helicopter dipped, bringing her out of her musings. She clutched the blanket to her neck, hoping to break the chill that still had an icy hold on her. How could she be so cold when the air was so hot she found it difficult to breathe? Her back hurt. She must have pulled something when she slipped while climbing out the attic window.

The man across from her extended his arm, embracing the woman huddled beside him. Abby felt a tug on her heart as the woman leaned her head against his shoulder and watched as the man lifted his free hand to the woman's face, wiping her tears away with his thumb. This wasn't a show; the man truly cared for his wife. Abby knew this to be true, as the woman neither flinched nor pulled away from his touch.

Abby swallowed. There was a time she'd not been afraid of Jacob. That lack of fear evaporated on their wedding day when he climbed out from behind the mask he'd been wearing and revealed himself to be a monster. No, worse than a monster; he was *'Il est le fils du diable—* the son of the Devil. Her thoughts drifted to Eva Radoux, the voodoo priestess who'd tried to warn her that the man she was marrying had a black heart. If only Abby had been able to understand the woman, she never would have married Jacob. Abby had told herself that countless times, but as she considered it now, she knew it was a lie. In the final moments of his life, Jacob admitted to the evils she'd uncovered only hours before, further admitting that he'd killed everyone who had ever cared for her and, in doing so, had controlled the narrative of her life since birth. It was obvious she was not a match for him. Even if she had been able to understand the woman, Jacob would have found a way to convince her the Cajun woman was senile. That would have been enough.

The thought made her lips quiver. The man had a silver tongue and was the king of manipulation in that lying was an art form he had perfected. She would have believed him, just as she always had in the past and just as she had when he'd translated the woman's words, telling her the woman was upset that she was marrying an older man. It should have been enough, and yet it wasn't. Jacob had to control the narrative, and that narrative ended with the woman being killed. Not by Jacob's hands, but her blood was on his hands just as sure as if he'd been the one to slit her throat. A wave of nausea washed over her. Her whole life had been a lie. She swallowed the bile that threatened.

Eva had been right—Jacob was the son of the Devil. He had to be; it was the only explanation for the way he'd treated her during their short, volatile marriage. Abby used the blanket to wipe the tears that sprang from her eyes. "It's okay, Abby, he can't hurt you anymore," she whispered in an effort to console herself. She swallowed the lies she told herself as another wave of nausea threatened. She didn't believe Jacob could no longer hurt her any more than she believed she would be able to get away with his murder. Jacob may have been the son of the Devil, but she was merely human, and even though she had acted out of desperation to protect both herself and the child she now carried inside, someone would have to pay for her sin.

Abby recalled her husband's final words, delivered in a moment of desperation, *"Even if I'm not here, they will find you."* The man was vile to his dying breath, sending out a warning she had no doubt was true. *"You may have won this round, but it's not over. Unless you die in this house with me, they will come after the child."* Jacob was dead, and even though he knew he was going to die, he carried the knowledge of who 'they' were to his watery grave with him. The realization brought on a new onslaught of tears.

Abby caught a shadow out of the corner of her eye and flinched.

"I'm sorry. I didn't mean to startle you."

Petty Officer Gomez? When did you get back? Abby looked to see there were two new people on board and realized the helicopter was now moving along at a fast clip. *Did I fall asleep again?* She didn't think so, but surely she would have noticed the new arrivals had she been fully awake. "I must have fallen asleep," she said, echoing her thoughts and explaining her actions.

Gomez nodded to the empty space next to her. "Mind if I sit?"

Abby took in the belly of the aircraft and realized the space was nearly full. How could she possibly refuse her rescuer a place to rest? She shrugged her indifference.

He sat down and handed her a headset and showed her how to use it. "No one else can hear our conversation."

Abby frowned. If the guy planned on making a move on her, she would have no choice but to throw him out of the helicopter. After all, she was going to face a murder charge; she might as well make sure it stuck. "And why do you think I would want to have a private conversation with you?"

Gomez bumped his shoulder against hers. "I'm not trying to hit on you or anything. I just thought maybe you'd like to talk to get your mind off things."

"Go ahead and talk. It's your aircraft," Abby replied.

He chuckled. "Technically, it belongs to the government; they just allow me to jump out of it from time to time."

Abby smiled a weary smile. "Lucky me." Funny, even though she'd been rescued, she didn't feel very lucky.

"You wouldn't have needed luck if you'd have evacuated before the hurricane," Gomez said, stating the obvious.

What was she supposed to say to that? Somehow, she doubted he would believe her if she told him the truth—that she'd wanted to leave, but a voodoo priestess told her she had to stay. Then again, if she hadn't heeded the woman's warning, she would not currently be worried about facing murder charges when the authorities figured out what she'd done. "I guess as long as there are people like me, then people like you will always have job security," she said with a shrug.

"I'm sorry about your husband," Gomez said softly.

"Me too," she lied.

Gomez sighed and placed his head against the skin of the aircraft. "Those bruises on your face look to be a few days old. Did he do that to you?"

Abby looked over at him and saw his eyes were closed. "Yes."

"It's probably a good thing he wasn't on the roof with you."

She was quiet for a moment until her curiosity got the better of her. "Why is that?"

"Because I would have rescued you first, and after seeing the bruises on your face, I may not have secured his harness as well as I should have."

His words surprised her. "I thought you were supposed to serve and protect?"

"No, ma'am, that is the police. I'm just a rescue swimmer. I get to punch people if they fight me."

"You think my husband would have fought you?"

Though his eyes were closed, a smile played at the edge of his mouth. "I would have made sure of it."

"You're pretty bold."

"Yes, ma'am. I'm a rescue swimmer," he said by way of explanation. He was quiet for several moments before speaking once more. "If anyone asks, your husband drowned."

Abby swallowed. "Of course, he drowned."

"I know."

Abby sat up and stared at him. "No, I mean he really drowned. You said that as if you don't believe me."

"Ma'am, I'm a guy. Not for nothing, but if I were in your husband's place, I would not have taken the chance of my wife and mother of my child slipping and falling when trying to make it to the roof. I would have gone out the window first and used my strength to pull you up after me. If I think that way, so will others. I'm going to ask you a question, and I need you to tell me the truth: was your husband alive when you climbed out that window?"

Abby suppressed a giggle. Not that she found his question funny; she always giggled when nervous. "Well, I didn't shoot him, if that's what you're asking."

"Good. So, if anyone asks, don't stop to think about their question. If they ask why you went up first, you tell them he told you to. Then, if they persist, you tell them you learned a long time ago not to question your husband's word. But to be honest, it is probably best just to parrot your initial response, saying your husband drowned."

"It's obvious you don't believe me, so why are you telling me all of this?"

"Because I don't blame you for whatever it was you did. My mom was in an abusive relationship for years, and it trickled down to us kids," he said without opening his eyes. I wish she had the guts to do what you did."

"My husband drowned," Abby said, allowing her voice to crack as she spoke.

Gomez smiled.

CHAPTER TWO

Kennedy approached Gomez and toed the sole of his boot with his own. Gomez opened his eyes; his hand moved to his headset. Abby knew he must have switched the channel as she watched his lips move without hearing what was said. Gomez nodded and immediately scrambled to his feet. He saw her looking and then brought his hand to his helmet. When he next spoke, she heard his words loud and clear. "Looks like you're going to have to hang out here just a little longer. The pilot saw something he wants us to investigate."

She nodded her understanding and started to tell him to be careful but stopped at seeing him switch the frequency once more. As she watched him strap himself to the guide wire, she wondered at the guts it took to exit a perfectly good—albeit loud—helicopter in mid-flight. There should be a medal for that. She fought the urge to roll her eyes at realizing this was the military and there most likely already was one. Not that she got the impression Gomez was doing any of this simply for the glory. While she didn't know him, she felt this was somehow more personal than a mere way to make a living. He'd said his mother was in an abusive relationship;

maybe this was his way of making up for not being able to help her. Great, she couldn't salvage her own life, and here she was playing Dr. Phil.

Gomez gripped the handle as the copter dipped to the left. Abby planted her feet to keep from sliding and felt a twinge of envy as the woman across from her grabbed her husband's arm, and despite the heat, he drew her close and kissed the top of her head.

Abby's eyes filled with tears as they drew comfort from one another. Her husband was dead. She had been instrumental in his death, and she couldn't figure out how she was supposed to feel. Relief seemed to top the list. But there was also a part of her that felt guilty for having blocked his escape. Knowing she was just as much responsible for his death as the water that infiltrated his lungs left her feeling hollow inside. She wasn't the kind of person who took joy in hurting others. She was the type that captured bugs from inside the house and released them outside instead of killing them, and yet here she was, a murderer! Her body succumbed to a tremble as she remembered.

The woman sitting across from her peered in her direction, staring at her as if she knew her secret. Abby blew out a breath, then dug her fingernails into the palms of her hands to keep from screaming at the woman, blasting her for passing judgment on things she had not witnessed. She hadn't set out to murder the man, but in the end, Jacob hadn't left her with another choice.

The helicopter stilled. Abby turned her attention back to the doorway where Gomez stood and watched as Kennedy fastened the wire to the harness and checked it to make sure it was secure before exchanging nods with Gomez. Next, Kennedy reached for the lever as Gomez shouted into the wind and stepped out as the cable lowered him from sight once more.

Abby sucked in a breath moments later when the cable returned empty, then relaxed when Kennedy hooked the end to a large metal basket and lowered it down again. Kennedy crouched in the opening with his hand on the lever, watching things she could not see. It didn't take long for the basket to return. Kennedy stood, then bent to guide the basket, which now played host to a dark-skinned woman with her arms tightly wrapped around a wide-eyed toddler. There was really no need for the woman to be holding the child so tight, as they were both strapped securely to the basket. Still, the woman held tight, protecting the child as only a mother could. Abby swallowed, wondering if she, too, would be successful in keeping her baby safe.

Kennedy unharnessed the basket, then, much to the child's displeasure, turned his attention to the door and lowered the guide wire once more. The next time it came up, Gomez was attached, his arms wrapped around a thin, shirtless man. After seeing them both safely on board, Kennedy turned his attention to the basket, unstrapping both the woman and the child, who tearfully raised his hands to the man who'd just come on board. Tears welled in the man's eyes as he scooped the child into his arms and held him as if afraid of losing him.

Watching the scene, Abby blinked back tears of her own as she placed her hand on her stomach, knowing her baby would always have that feeling of loss over never knowing its father. Anger welled inside as she realized the lies that surrounded her life would now trickle down to her child, who would also begin its life under the veil of lies. Bile rose in her throat as she wondered what kind of story she would invent that would turn a monster into a saint in her child's eyes and further wondered how she would keep from vomiting when having to repeat that lie over and over whenever the child asked. It wasn't fair. She was rid of him and yet would have to continue to live a life of lies while Jacob would be elevated to sainthood by a child who would never know the truth. But what if the child somehow discovered she was lying? Was she willing to have her child hate her as much as she hated Jacob for all he'd done to her?

A thought struck her that perhaps she should confess. At least if she went to prison, she would be able to tell the child the truth. And what would that solve other than allowing her to relate the story without it being a nauseating lie? The child would still be without a father and would possibly hate her despite her prison cell confession. *Calm down, Abby. You have time to decide.*

She looked at the toddler once more. Gleaming with sweat, he had his thumb wedged in his mouth, taking in his surroundings with the resilience of a child she believed to be no older than two—a child who would most likely grow up not recalling the events of the day. Even now, the boy sat on his father's lap, not knowing the why of what happened, only that he'd been hoisted up and was now safe within his father's arms.

Abby wondered how the family had ended up on the roof and doubted their story was any less harrowing than hers. At least she hadn't had to worry about dropping her baby as she climbed into the attic, scrambled through the narrow window, and made her way to the roof, all to protect the child. Okay, also to save herself, but she'd been spurred on by feeling the movement within her womb. And what would happen if she went to prison without any relatives to watch over the baby? Then, her child would be raised with strangers just as she had been. No, she couldn't do that to the baby. Not just any child, her child. A living being that would love her simply because she was its mother. She had to lie—if only to give her child something that was taken from her. Unconditional love. She would come up with a story and look into the mirror, saying it out loud until she could do so without being repulsed by the lie. She had time to get the story right and would see to it that the child believed every word. Besides, what was one more lie in the scheme of her life? Abby batted back tears. It was all too much to think about.

Gomez made his way back to where she sat and eased his way to the floor. "You look like you could use a friend."

"And you look ready to collapse," she said, wiping at her tears.

"Been a long few days," he agreed.

"Few days?"

"We flew in just after Katrina hit and were out rescuing people long before the levee was breached. Since then, we've been at it nearly nonstop," he said in a weary voice.

"Surely you're not the only one rescuing people?"

"No, ma'am, the sky is full of choppers. Squadrons from all over are here helping out with the aftermath. I came in from Houston, and they teamed me with Kennedy's crew to give their rescue swimmer a break."

"I would never have guessed you're not a member of the crew. You all work so well together," Abby replied.

"The Coast Guard training ensures that any Coast Guardsman can join any unit and seamlessly become a member of the team. I can take the place of any rescue swimmer on any base. It's the same with the whole crew. As you can see, it works well in an emergency situation,"

Gomez said, glancing at the passengers he'd saved.

"You must love your job."

"I love what I was trained to do, and I am damn good at it," he agreed.

"Why do I get the feeling there's a but in there?"

"Situations like this make it difficult to get much satisfaction out of doing my job. For every person I save, there are three more on the next roof, begging to be next. The chopper only holds so many, and some of them won't be there when we return. Some will get rescued; some will take it upon themselves to find another way, and many will drown or get infections from tainted water in the process," he said by way of explanation. "The hardest part of my job is living with the ghosts of those I couldn't save."

She recalled what Jacob had said about New Orleans being called the city of ghosts and realized the city would most certainly live up to its name. It dawned on her that she'd just thought of her husband and not recoiled. He'd had his moments. She made a mental note to draw from those moments when she was building the lie she would pass on to her child. The moment of respite was short-lived, as she knew from this moment on, she too would be living with a ghost of her own. She had a flash of memory of Eva Radoux, and her hand instinctively went to the bag that held the chicken foot. Make that ghosts.

"Do you really believe in ghosts?" she asked, thinking to tell him about the woman and Jacob's part in her demise. Abby looked at Gomez when he didn't answer. His eyes were closed, and she realized he'd fallen asleep. Barely more than a kid, he was doing a man's work. No, he was doing the work of many men. She glanced about the aircraft, noting each person on the helicopter who was not part of the crew, and smiled a slight smile. He might not be able to save them all, but it was not for lack of trying.

***

"We're landing." Gomez's voice floated in through the headphones, waking her. "Good luck out there."

Abby swallowed. "Out where?"

"Base camp. It's temporary. Once they get everything settled, they'll ship you off to an aid station, where they will help get you home—to family," he said before she could remind him her home was now underwater.

Abby frowned. "I don't have any family."

Gomez's brows knit together. "Mom, dad, uncle, distant cousin?"

Abby shook her head. "No." She started to add not that she knew of, but knew the response would lead to more questions, and she didn't want to saddle the man with things he had no business knowing.

"Not even one friend?"

She thought of Kevin for the first time since her rescue. That she hadn't thought of him before bothered her, since she'd entrusted her cat to the man. Gulliver. Had she not sent the feline with Kevin, she would very likely be dead, as she knew she would not have been able to leave him knowing he would surely drown, nor could she have gotten him to the roof by herself. Had the cat still been in the house, Jacob would have had all the leverage he needed either to keep her there with him or bribe his way onto the roof with her. How convenient it would have been for him to accidentally let go of the carrier on the way up to the roof. The thought of Gulliver floating away or, worse, being trapped in his carrier with no escape as it slowly filled with water was nearly too much to think of on its own. Knowing it bothered her more than listening to the man she'd married drown caused her to wonder at the monster Jacob had turned her into. How could someone so callous even think of raising a child? She didn't deserve to be a mother, nor did the baby she was carrying deserve to be raised by someone like her. A sudden wave of dizziness washed over her as she realized that her child might be better off if she did go to prison.

"Are you okay?" Gomez's voice was full of concern.

"Just a bit dizzy," she replied, then blew out a breath to calm the nausea that followed.

"Put your head between your knees," he suggested.

Feeling somewhat better, Abby cocked an eyebrow. "You're kidding, right?"

Gomez shrugged. "It's what they tell us to say."

She smiled a weak smile. "For future reference, I don't think you'll find many pregnant women who'll be able to accomplish that feat."

He glanced at the blanket that hid her stomach. "Point taken." He stood and reached out a hand to help her up.

"Thank you," she realized she didn't even know his first name, "Petty Officer Gomez."

His smile widened. "My friends call me Tom."

Her thoughts returned to her friend Kevin, the only person in her life she could really count on and a man who was overly fond of the name Tom. If only for missing the rescue, Kevin was going to be bummed that he had not remained in New Orleans to wait out the storm.

CHAPTER THREE

The last of the evacuees to leave the helicopter, Abby stepped off and into a sea of chaos. A line of tents ran as far as the eye could see. People in a variety of uniforms hurried about barking orders while others followed behind with clipboards, writing those orders down.

"Do you want me to walk with you to the intake tent?" Gomez asked, stepping up beside her.

Abby glanced at the helo, surprised to see the rest of the flight crew departing. "You don't have to go back up?"

"Soon. We've been on for hours. We'll get about a twenty-minute break before heading back out."

"Only twenty minutes?"

Gomez shrugged. "Places to go and people to save. The pilot and copilot will switch out."

"And you'll switch with Kennedy?"

"Nope. I'm the only one who gets to have that much fun."

Abby raised an eyebrow. "Fun?"

Gomez smiled and pointed at a patch on the front of his jumpsuit. "I'm a rescue swimmer. It's my job." Only the word job came out as "yob," and Abby knew he was making a joke.

She smiled. "And one you enjoy."

Gomez winked. "Just think of me as your knight in shining armor."

Abby was reminded of the fact that she'd once thought Jacob capable of filling that role. She started to tell Gomez she no longer believed in such things but was too tired for the discussion sure to follow. Instead, she smiled a weary smile and hoisted her purse across the front of her body to keep it safe. "Get some rest, Gomez. I'm sure I can find the intake tent on my own."

"Godspeed, Lady," he said, then raised his hand to capture his friend's attention and jogged off to catch up with the rest of the flight crew. Feeling more alone than ever, Abby fell into line behind the rest of the evacuees who had shared her helicopter. She and others who were arriving were funneled into a building-sized tent filled with people who glistened with sweat and sat on the ground watching the newcomers with nary a smile. Abby rubbed at the small of her back. After sitting on the hard surface of the chopper for so long, she'd been hoping to find a chair. She saw a woman in the late stages of pregnancy sitting on the ground with a small child in her lap. A man sat close by, rubbing the woman's swollen feet.

She sighed. *Suck it up, Abby; the only chair you're going to get is the electric chair. Or at least a prison cell with a shared toilet.* Normally, just the thought of a bathroom would send her out in search of one. She realized that while she'd been given water on the helo, she did not have to go. Further spurred on by the realization she no longer deserved any of life's luxuries, she found an open space and lowered to the ground. Keeping her purse slung across her body, she placed it in her lap to keep it secure. Staring at it, she realized that if she'd worn it like this the day she and Jacob walked the streets of New Orleans, perhaps she wouldn't have been such an easy target, and maybe she wouldn't have rushed into the marriage. She laughed at the thought, then looked around to see if anyone was watching. Luckily, everyone seemed to be too caught up in their own worries to pay heed to a pregnant woman who'd suddenly taken leave of her senses.

As the day wore on, more and more refugees filed into the tent. As they did, the stench of unwashed, sweat-laden bodies became overwhelming. When she'd first entered the tent, there was plenty of room to spread out, but now, Abby couldn't spread her arms apart without touching someone. Though she'd never considered herself claustrophobic, it suddenly felt as if the tent walls were closing in, and with that feeling, it seemed to bring every living soul inside on top of her. She could hear every breath, taste every odor, and feel every ache of those surrounding her. Abby pulled herself to her feet, watching as the woman who'd been sitting next to her moved into the empty space. Stepping over limbs attached to bodies that were sprawled out in every direction, she made her way to the opening and sucked in the humid air. She ran her hands through her hair, which was dripping with sweat, then slung her purse to the side and pulled at her top, which clung to her skin, revealing the early bump of pregnancy.

"You too?" a woman's voice asked.

Abby jumped, then trailed her eyes over the woman who appeared to be at least twenty years her senior. Mindless of her age, the woman wore shorts that covered little and a tank top that covered even less. Her long, curly hair was badly in need of a brush, her bare feet gave way to slender toes, and a dragon tattoo stretched across her right foot, rising up well above her ankle. Abby realized she was staring and lifted her gaze to meet the woman's eyes. "Me too?"

"Decided to take your chances out in the heat," the woman said by way of explanation. "It stinks to high heaven in there. At least here, there's a breeze. You looking for the bathroom?"

Abby shook her head.

The woman frowned then peered at Abby's stomach. "I ain't met a pregnant woman yet that didn't have to pee. Heck, when I was pregnant, I had to pee the second I got done peeing. You are pregnant, aren't you?" she asked, lifting her gaze.

Abby looked at the small mound that bulged beneath her top. "Yes."

The woman blew out a sigh. "Good. I thought I'd put my foot in my mouth. Wouldn't have been the first time. How far along are you?"

"Almost five months."

"Boy or girl?"

Abby shifted under the scrutiny of the questions. "I don't know. It was too early to tell at my last appointment. We were supposed to find out next week." Abby stretched and rubbed at the small of her back.

The woman laughed and waved a hand toward the tents. "I doubt you're going to make it to a doctor's appointment anytime soon. The way things look, we'll still be here next week. That purse looks heavy. It can't be good for your back. Maybe you should take it off."

Abby pulled her purse in front of her and eyed the woman closer. "My purse is none of your concern."

"Easy, sister. I'm not trying to rob you. I just think it is a bit suspicious that you don't have to go to the bathroom and now your back is hurting. It is hurting, isn't it?"

Abby wasn't sure what the woman meant by saying her back hurting was suspicious. What was suspicious was the woman's unrelenting questions. "I'm fine."

"What does the pain feel like?" the woman pressed.

"Just a bit of cramping. Nothing a good, soft chair wouldn't help," Abby said, brushing her off. Great, the woman was trying to help, and she was pushing her away. Perhaps if she had thought to ask questions of her own, she might have seen through Jacob's lies. If she would have run when she'd had the chance, she wouldn't be in this situation in the first place. Even as the thought came to her, she knew it was untrue. She was no match for Jacob and never had been.

Not true, she reminded herself. She'd done what was needed to protect herself and the baby, and because of that, she was the one standing here now, not Jacob. Just thinking of her husband made her skin crawl. If alive, he would not be happy that she was standing here talking to a complete stranger and would take pleasure in ordering Merrick to kill her like he'd done when she'd spoken to Eva the day he took her to the French Quarter. Relax, she told herself. Merrick is dead, and so is Jacob. And yet, here she was, still living in fear of both men.

Damn you, Jacob Buckley! I hope you rot in hell for everything you've done to me and those I love. She started to shake despite herself. That the woman hadn't questioned her words let her know she hadn't said them out loud. "Thank you for your concern, but I'm fine."

"I don't think so," the woman pressed. "You're pale as a ghost."

"I'm a redhead. I…"

The woman took a step forward and raised her hand.

Instinct took over, and Abby jerked to duck the impact.

As she did, her ankle rolled, sending her to the ground with a thud. Panic set in as a deep chill spread through her. Something was terribly wrong. It was too hot outside for her to be this cold.

The woman dropped to her side, brushing the hair from her face. "You're going to be okay."

"No, I'm not," Abby sobbed. "I will never be okay again!"

***

Abby stretched her legs, enjoying the coolness of the sheet against her skin, and breathed a sigh of relief. A dream—just a wicked bad nightmare. She opened her eyes, expecting to see Gulliver perched someplace close, and let out a frustrated sigh at seeing she was in a hospital bed. Not a dream. Not even a true bed, but a gurney in a small space cordoned off by curtains that hung from a silver rail attached to the ceiling. *An ER? How did I get here?* She started to move her arm and realized her wrists were tied to the metal rails on either side of the bed. She lay there for a moment, recalling the recent events of her life. The hurricane. The flood. Climbing into the attic to get away from both the water and Jacob. Jacob. He was so angry with her and had threatened to…

A chill ran through her. Then she remembered moving the large chest so he couldn't get to her. It was so heavy, but she'd managed to move it with ease. The bullets. He'd tried to kill her! Then it was she who'd succeeded in killing him. She pulled against the restraints which held her arms in place. "They know."

A dark-skinned woman wearing maroon scrubs appeared from behind the curtain. "Know what?"

Abby remained silent as the woman approached the bed.

The woman stood next to her bed. "Do you know your name?"

"Of course, I know my name. What kind of question is that?"

"The kind that lets me know if I can take the restraints off or not."

She was a murderer. Why would they remove the restraints? "My name is Abigail. Abby," she corrected. The only one who called her Abigail was Jacob.

"My name is Celie; do you know where you are?"

"A hospital?"

"Good. Let's get those things off you."

Abby worked to keep her expression neutral. Her secret wasn't out. At least not yet.

Celie nodded, moved to the bed and worked at the straps that held Abby's hands in place. When finished, she pulled back the sheet, lifting Abby's gown to adjust a belt that was fitted around her lower abdomen. She tugged at a wire and reattached it to the belt. "You are in the ER and look a might sight better than when you arrived last night."

"Last night?" Abby glanced at the monitor. "My baby?"

"You were severely dehydrated when you came in. You tried to pull out your IV, and nothing you said made any sense. You've been getting IV fluids, which appear to be working. Her heart rate was slow when you came in, but she seems to be doing much better now. It's not where we want it just yet, but it's getting there."

Tears welled in Abby's eyes. She'd wanted a little girl and even prayed it to be true as, in her mind, a boy was more likely to share his father's traits. Still, she was afraid to get her hopes up. "I'm having a girl?"

Celie sighed. "You didn't know?"

"No."

Celie shrugged. "Sorry to let the cat out of the bag if you were planning on it being a surprise."

"No, it's fine. It was too early before. We were supposed to find out at our next appointment."

"We?"

Abby faked a frown. "My husband and I."

"I would ask for his number, but the phone service is still down in New Orleans."

"My husband is dead," Abby said and allowed her bottom lip to quiver as she spoke. "The flood. He didn't make it out of the house. I had to climb to the roof." She shuddered, remembering.

"Is that how you got your bruises?"

Abby recalled her conversation with Gomez and how he'd known the bruises were old. If he knew, then Celie would know as well. She shook her head and lowered her eyes. "No, my husband did this to me. Dinner wasn't on the table in time," she said, hoping to gain the woman's sympathy. Abby raised her gaze. "My purse?"

Celie paused what she was doing and looked Abby in the eye. "That purse and everything in it is locked in the cabinet at the nurses' station. I was on when you came in and didn't think you'd want it just lying out in the open for anyone to walk off with it."

"You looked inside?"

"You were delusional when you arrived. I was looking for an ID. What were you thinking walking around with that much money?"

Abby considered her words as she looked at the diamond ring on her finger. "I was planning on leaving my husband. I purchased a zirconia ring that matched the one he'd given me and hocked the real ring."

Celie raised an eyebrow. "He didn't notice the swap?"

He would have if, in fact, she'd done what she claimed. Jacob was a control freak. With his attention to detail, he would have been quick to notice the discrepancy. Abby shook her head. "No, he didn't pay that close of attention to things like that."

"Maybe you're better off without the bastard," Celie mused.

While Abby agreed with her, she needed to remove all doubt. "I wanted to leave him. I didn't want him dead. I mean, what am I supposed to tell my daughter?" Just voicing that she was having a girl brought tears to Abby's eyes. Happy tears, which she squeezed from her eyes to add conviction to her words.

Celie sat on the bed and wrapped her arms around her. Suddenly, Abby wasn't pretending anymore. Her tears gave way to gut-wrenching sobs as she finally allowed herself to mourn the loss of her parents, Brian and Ned, and in a detached way, Jacob, who, until a few months ago, was the one person in her life who'd been there for her. Suddenly, anger fueled the tears as she clutched on to the woman sitting beside her and allowed the grief to evolve into uncontrollable sobs as she mourned a life of lies.

"It's okay," Celie said softly when Abby finally stopped crying. "I know it doesn't seem so now, but you are going to be okay."

It felt good to release all the sorrow she'd been harboring. But doing so opened her mind to her current dilemma. "I don't know what I'm supposed to do or where I'm supposed to go."

Celie stood and walked to the chair. When she returned, she held out the charm bag Eva's sister Pearl had given her for protection. "A chicken's foot is said to be powerful magic," Celie said when Abby took the pouch.

Abby gripped the small cloth pouch, feeling calmer as the pouch grew warm in her hands. "That's what Pearl said."

Celie sighed and rubbed her arms. "Pearl?"

Abby frowned. "You've heard of her?"

"No, but I was afraid you were going to tell me it was given to you by a woman named Eva Radoux. I had a crazy dream the other night where the woman came to me and told me I was supposed to help you. I didn't remember all the details of the dream until I saw the chicken foot yesterday." A blush crept up the woman's face. "I peeked inside the pouch after it fell out of your pocket when you were changing into your gown."

Abby looked at the pouch. "She called me by name?"

Celie shook her head. "No, she just showed me the chicken foot. But it is all just a silly coincidence anyway since she's not the woman who gave it to you."

"Eva Radoux was Pearl's sister," Abby said, clutching the bag tighter. She waited several moments, letting her words sink in before adding, "She was a voodoo priestess. She's been coming to me in my dreams ever since my husband had her killed."

Celie studied her with rounded eyes. "If your husband murdered her, why is she protecting you?"

"Had her murdered," Abby clarified. "I've asked myself that a million times, but I haven't got a clue. I just know my husband had her killed, and her sister showed up in the grocery store and gave me this."

Celie raised her hands, marking the sign of the cross, shaking her head as she backed toward the curtain. "Oh, hell no. This here is some voodoo shit, and I can't be part of no voodoo shit."

Abby watched the woman disappear behind the curtain

and prayed Celie wasn't heading out to call the police. Abby wasn't a religious person—not that she didn't believe in anything; more like she'd never known what to believe in. While voodoo might not be something most would turn to for comfort, it was the only thing she had. Sandwiching the pouch in her palms, she brought her hands to her face in prayer. "Please. I'm not sure why you are helping me, but you've gotten me this far; tell me what I'm supposed to do now."

CHAPTER FOUR

Abby heard voices in the hall. A moment later, a lanky woman with cropped hair and glasses pushed the curtain aside. Wearing khaki pants and a blue-collared shirt, the woman glanced at the clipboard she was holding. "Abigail Turner?"

"Turner?" Abby asked, wondering why the woman was using her maiden name.

The woman glanced at the clipboard once more. "You're not Abigail Turner?"

"It was the name on your driver's license," Celie said, stepping inside the curtain.

"I was." Abby heaved a sigh. Though she'd only been married to Jacob for a little over six months, she was so detached from her previous life that it seemed like a lifetime ago. "My married name is Buckley."

"Buckley," the woman repeated, lowering her pen to the clipboard.

Abby second-guessed her correction when Celie gave her a pointed look and shook her head. Oh well, what was done was done.

The woman with the clipboard drew her attention. "Have you been in contact with your husband since you've been here? I'm sorry. My name is Susan Taylor. I'm with FEMA. I'm responsible for collecting information from the evacuees at this hospital and working to help reunite you with your family."

"Mrs. Buckley's husband did not survive the hurricane," Celie answered for her. "She's been quite distraught since her arrival."

"He drowned," Abby said softly and allowed her bottom lip to quiver.

Susan frowned and wrote on the clipboard once more. "I am so sorry to hear that. What about other family, parents perhaps?"

Abby shook her head. "I lost both my parents last year."

"In-laws? Siblings? Anyone we can call?"

"I'm afraid Abby here doesn't have anyone. She only recently moved to the area to be with her husband and hasn't had a chance to meet anyone since arriving," Celie said.

Funny, while true, she didn't actually recall having this conversation with the woman. She started to mention Kevin when Celie caught her attention and gave a subtle shake of the head.

"What is your address?" Susan asked.

Abby waited for Celie. When the woman didn't seem to object, she spoke. "421 Dumas Street. New Orleans."

Susan nodded. "You said your husband drowned."

"Yes."

"You saw him?"

Abby waited for Celie to interject. "No," she said when she didn't.

"Then there is a chance he survived." Susan's voice was hopeful.

Abby felt her heart rate quicken as her hands went to

her stomach. *Jacob's dead. He has to be.* When she spoke, her voice did little to hide her fear. "I don't think so. The water was coming into the house, and Jacob didn't make it into the attic with me," she said, leaving out the part where she moved the chest over the opening to prevent him from following.

"Presumed dead," Susan said and scribbled something on the paper. She lifted the pen and smiled a weak smile. "Miracles do happen. We will flag the address and send a crew in as soon as it is safe to do so."

"You're not trying to say you think he could still be alive inside the house? The water was clear to the attic." Abby's voice trembled as she spoke.

"No, that is not at all what I'm saying. But we could perhaps hope he managed to get outside and swim to safety. If not, it would be more of a body recovery mission so we can officially list him as deceased." Susan heaved an audible sigh. "I'm afraid there will be many such missions."

Abby nodded her agreement.

"It is my understanding you will be staying for a few days. Either I or someone else will check in on you before you go." She stood and clutched the clipboard to her chest. "In the meantime, do you need anything?"

"A cell phone?" Abby said, then regretted her comment when Celie's jaw tightened.

Susan tilted her head. "You just told me you have no one to call."

Abby allowed her lip to tremble once more. "You're right. I am so used to having it with me that I wasn't thinking."

Celie walked to the head of the bed and fiddled with the IV machine. "Abby was severely dehydrated when she came in. She's also been given something to settle her nerves. It seems her mind is still a bit jumbled."

"It's perfectly understandable. The poor thing has been through a great ordeal." Susan was nearly to the curtain when she stopped and spun around. "Just out of curiosity, Mrs. Buckley, why didn't you and your husband evacuate before the hurricane hit?"

Abby thought of her conversation with Jacob while watching the news of Katrina's path. "My husband lived in New Orleans for twenty-seven years and was convinced it was all just hype."

"I guess he was wrong," Susan retorted.

Taking exception to the woman's tone, Abby narrowed her eyes at the woman. "The authorities said the levee would hold. We had no reason to believe our government would lie to us." That she was defending Jacob pissed her off enough to produce tears, which worked in her favor.

"I'm sorry. I didn't mean to upset you," Susan said and left without waiting for a response.

Celie held up a finger to her lips, then went to the curtain and peeked into the hallway. "I don't think you'll be seeing her again," she said, returning to the bed.

"Good," Abby said, wiping her eyes.

"That was a good show. It looked as if you really cared for the jerk."

"There was a time when I did," Abby said softly. "I do have a friend."

"I'm sure you have plenty of friends, but she doesn't need to know where to find you unless you want to be found." Celie crossed herself once more. "Listen, I still don't like all this voodoo stuff, but I remembered something else the woman said."

"The FEMA Lady?"

"No, the one from my dream. The voodoo lady. She said, 'No trust stranger.'"

Abby's mouth went dry as she looked toward the opening of the curtain, half expecting to see Nathan Riggs standing there. While the man had seemed charming at first, he was no different than Jacob, who'd wagered with the man to test her loyalty. She tore her gaze away from the curtain and looked at Celie. When she spoke, her voice trembled. "Are you sure that's the stranger she was speaking of?"

Celie shrugged. "I don't know. Why?"

Abby ran her hands along her arms. "I need to leave. It's not safe here."

"I'll go check to see what's holding up your transfer."

"Transfer?"

"To your room. They'll be moving you as soon as it's ready."

Abby reached to pull the IV from her arm. Celie grabbed hold of her hand and nodded to the covers. "Unless you're prepared to yank out that catheter as well, you'd better leave that in place."

Okay, that explained a lot, including why she hadn't felt the need to go to the bathroom. "It's not safe here."

"Don't let what that woman said get to you. You said it yourself, there's no way he could have gotten out of the house," Celie said.

Everything in her being knew that to be true, but it didn't stop that seedling of doubt that had been planted. And then what of Eva's words, which had nearly echoed those of her sister? *No trust the stranger.* Words that clearly showed she and her baby weren't out of danger yet.

Celie's voice cut through her thoughts. "Listen, you have to think about your baby. She was unstable when you

Sinister Winds

came in."

"My baby? You said she is doing better."

"She is, but we need to monitor you both a little longer just to make sure everything is okay."

"It's not safe," Abby repeated.

"You're just nervous because there aren't any walls and anyone and their brother can stick their head around the curtain. You'll be much more comfortable in the maternity ward. And don't you worry, they take security very seriously up there. No one comes in or out without being screened."

"Will you still be my nurse?" Abby asked.

Celie shook her head. "No, I work the ER, but Roberta, the lead nurse on the floor, is my best friend. If it is okay with you, I'll tell her about my dream."

Feeling Celie had probably already confided in the woman, Abby managed a smile. "I guess she wouldn't be considered a stranger if she's your best friend."

Celie bobbed her head in agreement. "Great, plus I'll check on you from time to time. Now, let me go check on your transfer status. Do you need anything else?"

"A telephone?" Abby said sheepishly.

"I'll see what I can do, but not until you get upstairs where there's less chance of you'll be overheard," Celie said and disappeared around the curtain.

Left alone with her thoughts, Abby turned to her side and focused on the machine that monitored the baby's heart rate. Watching the line rise and fall while counting the beats, she placed her hands on her abdomen. "Hang in there, little one; Momma's working to keep you safe," she said, then pulled her feet up and closed her eyes.

"Knock knock," a man's voice called out as the curtain slid along the metal rail. She felt more than heard him enter the room and knew the greeting was more a formality than an expectation of being welcomed into the room.

Abby turned to see a man who looked to be in his early twenties, with golden brown arms and straight, brilliant white teeth, standing at the edge of her bed. *Oh, Kevin would love you,* she thought. That she hadn't thought to claim him for herself spoke merits.

He moved to the side of the bed, unhooking wires and pulling the bags from the IV pole as he spoke. "Sir Albert Nuez, at your service, my lady."

Okay, so not the name she'd expected, but at least he was polite.

"I've come to take you to your room. There's no use looking around for a chariot. You're already in it. We'll switch you out to a more comfortable model once we get you to your room." He walked to the chair and gathered her clothes, placing them in a white plastic bag, which he then placed on the end of the gurney by her feet. He looked about the room. "No shoes?"

Abby craned her neck, searching the nearby floor. Not seeing any, she searched her mind, wondering if she'd been wearing any when she went to the roof. For the life of her, she couldn't remember. She shrugged.

"Not to worry. I'll be back in a jiff," he said, leaving the space.

Celie came into the curtained area several moments later carrying Abby's purse. "I don't reckon you'll be wanting to leave this down here."

"No, I don't suppose I would," Abby said, clutching it to her chest. "The cell phone?"

Celie shook her head. "Not yet. You should have a phone in your room, but I'm not sure you'll be able to call long distance. I could probably get you a prepaid one and bring it up to you."

Abby reached into the purse and pulled out a hundred-dollar bill. "Will this cover it?"

"And then some," Celie told her.

"Okay, maybe you can get me some shoes too? Size seven. Albert looked but didn't see any."

Celie smiled. "You met Albert."

"I met him, and I assure you I'm not interested."

"Good, because he's gay."

Abby thought of Kevin once more and smiled.

"Not the reaction that comment usually gets," Celie told her.

"Just thinking of my friend Kevin, also gay. He's going to be so bummed he left town and missed all the fun."

Celie laughed. "You have a warped sense of fun."

"I assure you, Kevin would be in heaven not only with Albert but by all the rescuers too."

"It's probably for the best he's not here. Albert has a boyfriend. The dude really hit the jackpot, as Benji is even cuter than he is," Celie said with a sigh.

Before Abby could comment, Albert returned with a pair of thick yellow socks. "Okay, Princess, out with the feet."

Abby stuck her foot out and watched as Albert ran his fingers firmly along her ankles for several moments, then placed the sock on her foot. She looked at Celie, who smiled a knowing smile, then stuck out the other foot as he lowered the first and picked up the second sock.

He took the time to massage the ankle, then covered it as well. Albert smiled. "My sister is pregnant; I know a thing or two about swollen ankles."

The heck with Kevin, Abby mused, rethinking her original thought. *I want you all for my own.* Not that she was interested in anything more than having him rub her feet.

Albert pointed at her purse. "Are you sure you don't have a pair of shoes stashed in there?"

"I'm sure," Abby said, clutching the bag tighter. Worried he'd further question the bulk of the bag, which was loaded with the cash she'd found hidden in Jacob's office before her escape, she shrugged. "To be honest, I couldn't tell you what all is in here. I saw the water coming into the house and just started cramming stuff inside. I guess I was in panic mode because it's mostly stuff I thought the baby would use." Okay, not a total lie.

Celie moved up beside the bed. "She wasn't wearing any shoes when she came in."

Something about the comment bugged her. Then again, her mind wasn't the clearest at the moment.

"You two best be going," Celie said, stepping aside. "They're shipping us more patients, and we are going to need the bed."

"Come on, fair maiden," Albert said, pushing the bed forward. "We've been kicked out of the lair. If we're lucky, we shall find you a room with a view."

"I'll settle for a room with walls," Abby said as they passed through the curtain.

"Oh, well, in that case, I am sure we can find something suitable." He maneuvered the hospital bed through the ER and into a wide hallway. He stopped in front of the elevator and pushed the up button. The door opened almost immediately. Albert pushed the bed inside and pushed a button on the panel.

"Do you know what you are having?" he asked as the doors closed.

"A little girl," Abby replied.

"Do you have a name picked out?"

Abby shook her head. "No." Each time she brought it up, Jacob had refused his input, saying they had plenty of time to worry about the details. It struck her as odd at the time that a man as meticulous as Jacob was so blasé when it came to naming their child. Never in a million years could she have guessed the reason for his indifference, that money meant more to him than having a child born of his blood.

"My sister is naming her child Clennie Cloyce," Albert said, interrupting her thoughts.

Abby looked over at the man. "You're kidding, right?"

Albert placed his hand on his chest and then palmed the air as if willing her to believe him. "Girl, I wish I was. Can you imagine what her life is going to be like in fourth grade?"

Abby raised an eyebrow. "Only fourth grade?"

"I find fourth grade to be a turning point in a kid's life. Sixth grade is even worse."

"Spoken like someone who knows."

"Received my first kiss and my first heartache in the sixth grade. Bonnie Sue Crawford was the cutest girl in school. That rejection made me what I am today."

"Does she know she turned you gay?" Abby asked.

He laughed and shook his head. "Girl, you don't make someone gay. I was already gay, and Bonnie Sue knew it. She was just playing along so I could make Carl Horst jealous. I thought that maybe he was gay but wasn't sure, and it's not like you can just walk up and ask a kid that kind of thing. The plan was to have her kiss me so I could judge his reaction. Only I didn't count on how good of a kisser Bonnie was, and it went on a bit longer than either of us expected. The moment we stopped, Carl walked over, and instead of professing his love, he punched me in the nose."

"Punched you in the nose! Why?"

"It turns out I had Carl pegged wrong. He wasn't hanging around me because he liked me; he was hanging around because I was friends with Bonnie."

Abby worked to keep from laughing. "And Carl liked Bonnie."

"Yep, I may have been born gay, but it took years to perfect my gaydar."

Abby laughed. "Wait, you said the rejection made you what you are today. How?"

"Because Carl Horst could throw a punch. My nose bled so much that my mom thought I was going to bleed to death. She took me to the ER, and my nurse ended up being…"

"Gay?" Abby asked.

Albert chuckled. "I have no idea. As you recall, my gaydar was not honed back in the day. But he was a guy, and he was good at his job. And from that moment on, I knew that was what I wanted to do." Albert smiled a brilliant smile. "My family isn't really the college type. So, I have to put myself through nursing school. I go to school by day and work here in the evenings and on weekends. When I graduate next spring, I will be working here as a nurse full-time and will have done it all on my own." The elevator dinged as it came to a stop. The doors opened, and she and Albert were on the move once more.

As he rolled her to her room, Abby thought of her own life. She'd had plans of going to college, and then she'd married Brian. She'd thought about going to night school, and Brian had thought it was a good idea, but then he was dead. Shortly after losing him, she'd lost both her parents and needed a life ring. Perhaps if she'd had something to aspire to, she might not have been desperate enough to think of Jacob as the only solution to her problems. She waited until they were in the room, and she could look him in the eyes. "Good for you, Albert."

His face turned serious. "I like to think that I, too, may be an example for someone else someday."

"You already are, Albert. You're a real class act. You just make sure to keep true to yourself and don't ever let anyone destroy that fire."

"No, ma'am. Ain't no one going to put this baby in a corner," he said with a wink.

While she'd been prepared to answer a barrage of questions, there were none forthcoming, and for that, she was grateful.

CHAPTER FIVE

Much to Abby's delight, she now occupied a single occupancy room complete with walls, a door, and a locker to stow her purse. While the window didn't offer much of a view, it was rather large and allowed plenty of sunshine to fill the space. While she'd still not been allowed out of bed to take a shower, the continuous fluids being pumped in through the IV in her arm had her feeling better than she'd felt in days. Physically, at least. Mentally, she was still at war with herself over what she'd done. As she sat listening to the monitor beside the bed that tracked her baby's heart rate, she fought the urge to pick up the hospital phone and call Kevin. She knew the man had to be beside himself with worry but feared the conversation would turn to things best spoken about on phones that couldn't be listened in on. She would wait until Celie brought the cell phone she'd promised.

Abby turned on the television and was immediately immersed in news reports regarding Hurricane Katrina. Tears trickled down her cheeks at seeing the severity of the damage and the enormity of the flooding. While she'd known it to be bad, she hadn't known just how bad until seeing the footage. Houses were gone, multi-story hotels ripped from their foundations, and yachts lay capsized in the middle of the street. The report switched to the area where she and Jacob lived, showing the houses submerged in coffee-colored water. A chill raced up her spine when the reporter stated there were reports of snakes and alligators swimming in the murky water.

The scene changed to a helicopter rescuing a family from the roof. Abby thought of Gomez, Kennedy, and the crew and wondered how they were faring. It dawned on her that there could be footage of her rescue on the news as well. She turned up the volume and listened as a different reporter told of the trouble in the Coliseum and of evacuees being without water and basic supplies needed. A person being interviewed told of the violence she'd seen, then she shook her fist in the air and said the government should be ashamed of themselves.

Abby rubbed her arms as she recalled Jacob asking if she wanted to go to the Coliseum. She recalled Pearl's warning; she had repeated the last line with a tone that had held an eerie warning. *The only way you live. The only way your bebe is safe.* It struck her now that if not for Pearl's warning, she would have agreed to go. Abby turned off the television and placed the remote on the table. As she pulled her feet up and curled into a ball, she recalled Jacob's words. *Even if I'm not here, they will find you. It is the way things work. They paid good money for the child. Unless you die in this house with me, they will come after the child.* Abby prayed the man had only been messing with her mind. Pearl had seemed adamant that she and the baby would be safe if she followed her instructions. *The way up is the way out. Only one must go up. It's the only way.* Had the woman known the enormity of the words? Could she have known her advice would mean Jacob would die?

Abby shivered once more; of course she had. But what about what Jacob had said? Was he just trying to scare her, or did he know something Pearl didn't?

Abby splayed her hands across her stomach. "Don't worry." As the words came out of her mouth, she wondered if she was speaking to the baby or trying to comfort herself. Unable to find comfort in either her words or the television, she closed her eyes and allowed herself to give in to sleep.

Abby woke to find the room dark. Not only were the lights off, but the curtains were pulled closed with the only light entering the room coming from the hallway and via the machines near the bed. She struggled to remember if she'd closed the curtains, then further wondered if she'd slept the day away. As she became more aware of her surroundings, she knew without seeing that she wasn't alone in the room. Her heart rate increased as she scanned the dark confines of the room. Her gaze settled on the shadow of a person sitting in a chair near the window. Though it was dark, she could tell by the outline that the person was a man wearing a suit.

"Hello, Abigail." The voice was smooth.

Jacob. He's not dead. A mixture of fear and relief washed over her as she worked to push the cobwebs from her mind.

He rose and walked to the bed, but instead of approaching her, he walked to the other side. She followed him with her gaze, blinking in horror as he bent and lifted something from a cart beside the bed. Though her mind told her what that something was, she refused to believe it. She held her breath to keep from screaming as she fumbled for the bedside remote and turned on the lights.

He turned toward her, pulled back the blanket, and

Sinister Winds

showed her the infant he was holding. The baby wiggled in his arms, and she saw its red peach-fuzz hair.

"You made me a very happy man today, Abigail," Jacob said.

Her hands flew to her stomach, flat and devoid of child. How could that be and why couldn't she recall giving birth?

Jacob smiled. "Don't worry, my dear. You can always have another one."

"Another one? I don't understand."

"Your mind is a little fuzzy. I told you I had friends in high-reaching places. After that little stunt you pulled in the attic, I knew you couldn't be trusted, so I had the doctors sedate you until after you gave birth. I couldn't take a chance of having you run off again. Not when there was so much at stake. I would let you hold her, but that would not do well for your mental wellbeing. Besides, her parents are eager to meet her."

Abby started to get up and found that her hands were tied to the bed rails. She struggled against her restraints. "No, you can't take her."

Jacob laughed a haunting laugh, then took hold of Abby's chin and made her look at him. "Don't you see, Abigail, I already have. We are linked forever, and I will take what is mine again and again! You think about that while I am gone. I'll be back for you as soon as I hand off the delivery. When I do, we'll have a nice little chat about how you left me in the house to die."

"Jacob!" she screamed as he walked out of the room. "She's mine. You can't take her from me!" The door closed behind him, and the room grew dark once more.

Abby opened her eyes, saw the sun streaming into the room and felt a flutter of movement from the life within her. She felt her stomach and the distinct mound of her growing pregnancy. Tears welled in her eyes. It was only a dream.

She heard a faint click and looked to see a woman in white scrubs with pink and white teddy bears standing near the locker that held her purse.

Still reeling from the dream, Abby screamed at the woman. "WHAT ARE YOU DOING?!"

The woman turned and held up a shopping bag. "Celie asked me to give these to you."

"Stay out of my locker!" Calmer now, Abby lowered her voice, but it still held an edge.

"Take it easy. I wasn't trying to steal anything; I thought you were sleeping and didn't want to wake you," the woman said, closing the distance. "I'm Roberta, Celie's friend."

Abby took the bag she offered and worked to still her nerves. Opening the bag, she looked inside and breathed a sigh of relief at seeing the cell phone and a pair of adjustable sandals. "I was sleeping," she said, easing her tone. She wanted to add that she wished the woman had come in sooner and woken her from her nightmare, but it was too late for that now.

"Wow, and I thought I was a light sleeper," Roberta replied.

Abby thought to tell her she hadn't always been a light sleeper, that she'd developed the attribute as a survival technique to keep from being taken unaware by her deranged husband, but offered a shrug instead. The dream had rattled her. The last thing she wanted to do was talk openly about the man who was just as scary in death as he'd been in life. "New surroundings, I guess."

"That'll do it. I don't know many who can sleep in a

hospital bed."

Abby doubted she would do much more sleeping after the dream she'd just had. She glanced at the monitor. "Is my baby okay?"

Roberta stepped up to the monitor and watched the screen for several moments. "Everything looks just fine. Have you felt her move lately?"

Abby nodded. "I felt her a few moments ago. The first time since I've been in here."

"Good. It means the fluids are working. Speaking of which, you are almost out of saline. I'll change it out so you don't get an alarm in a few moments when the bag goes dry. Can I get you anything else? Fresh water and a snack, perhaps?"

Abby smiled. "Yes, please."

"Okay, I'll be back in a jiff."

As soon as Roberta left, Abby pulled the phone from the bag, fought her way through the packaging, and booted it up. She'd just finished loading it when Roberta returned with two small containers of orange sherbert, saltine crackers, and a mustard-yellow plastic pitcher of ice water, along with a clean cup.

"This should hold you until they bring you up a tray," Roberta said, setting the water and snacks on the bed tray. She pulled a clear bag of liquid from her pocket and went to work switching out the IV bag.

"Any idea when I'm going to get out of here?" Abby asked as she dipped her spoon in the sherbert.

"The baby's heartbeat is still a bit slow. It should get better as we get you rehydrated. I'd imagine you'll be with us a couple of days yet." She frowned. "From what Celie said, I took it that you had no place to go."

"I don't really." It wasn't that she wanted to leave, but

the room felt less safe now that she knew Jacob could visit her in her dreams.

Roberta started to speak, then stopped.

Abby sighed. "Celie told you about her dream, didn't she?"

Roberta nodded. "Don't go getting mad at the girl. She was pretty freaked out over it."

"You believe her?" Abby asked.

Another nod; this one came with a raised eyebrow. "Of course. We both grew up in New Orleans. Celie was more freaked out than me, but that's because my grandmother is a conjurer. As soon as Celie told me, I called Granny and told her. She said if the priestess told her to help you, then it was best we keep you safe or face the consequences."

"How can she do it?"

Roberta wrinkled her brow. "Do what?"

"Come to us in our dreams," Abby said, knowing the act to be more than a simple dream. Jacob was a dream and a bad one at that, but when Pearl or Eva visited, it was different. When she woke from the dream with Jacob, she knew it to be a dream, but with them, it was as real as talking to Roberta now. Abby waved her arms. "How does she know where I am or come to people in their dreams? How did she know I would be here? I mean, she had to know, or she wouldn't have known to have Celie look after me."

"Abigail, when it comes to voodoo, I've learned it's best not to ask too many questions."

Abby cringed at the use of her given name. "Please, call me Abby, and why not ask questions? Don't I deserve to know why she picked me? Besides, I have more questions. And since she seems to know everything that is going to happen, I'd like to figure out how to find her."

Sinister Winds

"If she wants you to find her, she'll make sure you do."

"All the same," Abby said, "please tell Celie if she talks to her again to tell her I'd like to speak to her."

"I'll be sure to pass it along," Roberta said, then eyed the bag. "Would you like me to put your shoes in the locker?"

Abby handed her the bag and watched the woman cross the room and place the bag in the bottom of the locker before shutting the door once more.

She turned and saw Abby watching. "Celie told me what you have in your purse. Not the amount, just that it is a lot. I know having that here has to worry you. I can bring you a lock if you want, or I can make it so you don't have to worry about it."

"How?"

"If I tell the other nurses about Celie's dream, they'll know you are protected. Stuff like that gets around, and won't no one dare bother you."

While tempting, Abby decided it best to stay below the radar. "I think a lock will do."

"Okay, suit yourself, but if you change your mind, let me know." Roberta walked to the window, took hold of the chain that maneuvered the window shade and frowned. "That sun's awfully bright. Do you want me to close the shades? They are room-darkening so that our new moms can sleep when their babies are resting. One pull of this chain, and it will be dark as night in here as soon as you turn the lights off."

Abby shuddered against an unseen chill. "No, I'd rather you leave them open if you don't mind."

"Okay. Just let me know if you change your mind," Roberta said as she released the chair and moved away from the window. "Oh, and Celie said to tell you there was a man asking about you earlier. She avoided his questions and told him you were released. Don't you go getting all worried because no one gets into this area without being vetted by one of my nurses."

"What did the man look like?" Abby asked as Roberta was leaving the room.

Roberta shrugged. "She didn't say. Only that he was good-looking and wearing a dark suit."

Abby started to tell Roberta about her dream when the woman's pager beeped, and she hurried from the room.

CHAPTER SIX

Abby's hands trembled as she punched Kevin's number into the phone and pressed to make the call. *Calm down, Abby; this is all just a crazy coincidence. Jacob's dead and cannot hurt you.*

"Hello?" The voice was deep.

For a moment, Abby thought she'd dialed the wrong number. "Kevin?"

"Abby?!"

This time, the voice was shrill and excited and more in line with the voice she'd been expecting. Tears of relief pooled in her eyes. "Kevin! It's so good to hear your voice."

"Same! You sound like you're crying. Are you alright? I've been beside myself with worry. What took you so long to call?"

Abby smiled and wiped at her tears. "I am crying, but just because it's so good to hear your voice. How's Gulliver?"

"Fat, sassy, and happy. The news is just awful. I was worried that…"

"I got out," she said, cutting him off. "I wanted to call, but I forgot my phone, and I just got another."

"And the Dick?" Kevin's tone showed his disgust for the man.

Abby struggled with the answer.

"Are you still there?" Kevin's voice was full of concern.

"I'm here, and until a few moments ago, I would've told you Jacob is dead, but now I'm not so sure. I mean, he has to be dead, but…"

"Okay, how about you start from the beginning?" Kevin offered.

"I thought Jacob drowned. I was able to get to the roof, but he was stuck in the house," Abby said, leaving out the details in between.

"What do you mean you were on the roof?"

"The water was coming into the house, and so I went to the attic. When the water came in there, I went out the window and stayed on the roof until I was rescued," she said, willing him to focus on that. While she wanted to tell him the rest, she didn't want to say anything that anyone could overhear.

"You're pregnant! What the Devil are you doing climbing out windows?" His voice softened. "You are still pregnant, aren't you?"

Abby glanced at the monitor, which showed the baby's heartbeat. "Yes, she is fine."

"She? We're having a girl?"

Abby laughed. "One of us is."

"Nope, you're not going to take this from me. I'm too invested now. I don't care if I get to be an aunt or an uncle, but I'm laying claim to protecting that baby girl right here and now, and I promise she'll never want for anything as long as Auntie Uncle Kevin is here."

Abby was surprised at how much talking to Kevin was

brightening her mood. "Okay, sorry, but that's just weird. You'll have to pick one and stick to it."

"Wait, how did you find out the baby is a girl?"

"We're okay, Kevin," Abby said, including the baby. "I'm in the hospital. I was a little dehydrated, and that caused the baby's heartbeat to be a little slow. The doctor said she was lethargic, so they are keeping me here for a couple of days just to be sure."

"Hospital? Which one? Not in New Orleans. They've evacuated everyone. Tell me which one, and I'll be on my way," Kevin urged.

Abby hadn't considered that she'd been moved to a different area. Still, while the offer was tempting, Abby wasn't willing to bring Kevin back into the fray without knowing for certain that Jacob was dead. She worked to keep the fear from her voice. "Don't be silly. The news says the flights are all delayed. I'll be out of the hospital before you even get here." *Wherever here is.*

"Then I'll drive."

"Kevin, you know I love you, but the answer is no."

"You're holding out on me," he said firmly. "Quit treating me like a baby you have to protect and tell me what's really going on."

Kevin was right. After all he'd done for her, he deserved to know the truth. "Okay. Jacob is dead; he has to be, as he didn't follow me onto the roof."

"Didn't or couldn't?" Kevin asked.

"We'll talk about the details later," she said, mentally willing him to understand her reluctance to speak about such things over the phone.

"Okay, so the poor thing perished in the flood," Kevin said, letting her know he understood her need for secrecy. "How'd you get off the roof?"

"Helicopter."

"Did they bring you up in a stretcher or strapped to a harness?"

"Harness." She started to tell him the man's name was Tom but knew he wouldn't hear another word after that.

"Girl! I know that had to be exciting."

"To be honest, I barely remember it."

"You're telling me you were hanging in mid-air strapped to a burly man, and you don't recall any of the details?" Kevin's voice was incensed.

Actually, even though she didn't consider Gomez burly, she did recall every single detail; she simply wasn't ready to relive it just yet. "I was dehydrated and riddled with grief, remember."

"Oh yeah. But I still don't understand why you think the Dick is alive. You said he wasn't on the roof with you, so that means he wasn't rescued. You don't think he managed to swim to safety, do you?"

"I didn't think so," Abby replied.

"What changed your mind?"

"A number of things."

"Sunshine, talking to you is like talking to a straight man who thinks every conversation is about me trying to turn him gay."

Abby laughed. "Isn't it?"

"Depends on what the man looks like, but that's beside the point," Kevin said with an extravagant southern drawl. "Now, unless that prepaid phone of yours comes with unlimited talk time, could you just tell me what you know without making me ask?"

"A woman came into the ER and said she was with FEMA. She asked a bunch of questions and then marked Jacob as presumed dead."

"Presumed? Surely, she doesn't think he's still alive."

"I don't know what she thinks, but she said without a body, she would have to mark him presumed dead."

"I can see her point. But that is just government bureaucracy and nothing for you to sink your teeth into."

"Okay, I admit that it gave me pause, but I didn't dwell on it. Then they transferred me to my room, and I had a dream." A chill washed over her. "Oh, Kevin, the dream was so real. I was sleeping, and when I woke up, Jacob was standing over me, holding the baby. He told me he'd paid the doctors to sedate me until after the baby was born. He had the baby and was taking her to her new home. He made it sound as if that was all I was to him—a baby-making machine, and he would take every baby away." She realized she was crying and wiped at her tears. "What if he's alive?"

"It was just a dream, Sunshine. Probably brought on by the doubts instilled by the woman from FEMA."

"That's what I thought too," Abby replied, "until Roberta, my nurse, told me there was a man in the ER asking about me. Kevin, she said he was wearing a suit. Jacob was wearing a suit in my dream. It can't simply be a coincidence."

"Sure it could," Kevin said, though his words lacked conviction. "Seriously, just tell me where you are, and I'll come get you."

"No," she said, leaving no room for argument. "This is my mess to clean up. Besides, Pearl knows I'm here."

"The voodoo priestess is there? Why didn't you say so?"

"I didn't say she was here. I said she knows where I am. The ER nurse freaked out when she realized it was me because she said she'd had a dream about me even before

I arrived. She said the woman told her that she was Eva. I'm assuming that Pearl knows too. It's crazy, I know, but it's true."

"It's not fair. How come everyone else gets visited by her in their dreams and not me? I mean, I was living right next to you. I helped, even though I knew the Dick might kill me, and does she come visit me? Nooo…wait, do you think she has something against gays?"

Abby laughed despite herself. "Maybe she hasn't visited you because she doesn't need to. You didn't help me because she scared you into doing so. You helped me out of the goodness of your heart. Do you know how much that means to me?" Abby said sincerely. "You're right. If Jacob had known you were helping, he would have had you killed." She stopped short of telling him that Jacob had found out about their friendship and had indeed promised to kill him.

Kevin giggled. "He'd have to find someone new to do his dirty work."

She knew Kevin was talking about the fact that Merrick was dead. "Yes, well, we'll leave that for a later discussion."

"You're forgetting you are calling from a prepaid phone," Kevin replied.

"You're forgetting you're not," Abby reminded him.

"Point taken. You said the voodoo woman visited the nurse in her dreams. What did she say?"

"She told her to protect me."

"And she believed her."

Abby raised a brow to the phone. "Wouldn't you?"

"*Touché.*"

"Don't ever use that word again!" Abby said a bit too heatedly. "I'm sorry, I didn't mean to snap. It's just that

Jacob used to say that."

"Are you okay?" Kevin asked.

"I will be. It just feels like I'm living with ghosts," Abby replied. "Jacob used to say New Orleans was the city of ghosts. He loved the city. I guess it's only natural he'd become one of them."

"Good, he can stay there when you leave. We don't have room for them here at this house."

Guilt washed over her as she realized she had yet to ask him how he was doing. "Oh, Kevin, I'm sorry. I was so caught up in my own stuff that I haven't even bothered to ask how you are doing."

"I'm good now that I know you're okay. You are okay, right?"

She smiled at the phone. "I think I needed to hear your voice just as much as you needed to hear mine."

"Why, Abby Buckley, I have half a mind to ask you to marry me."

Abby's smile widened. "If I weren't in mourning and you were not gay, I'd gladly accept. Heck, maybe I'll marry you anyway just to get rid of that last name. I wonder if it is too late to get an annulment."

"Probably wouldn't look good for a grieving widow," Kevin mused. "Give it a few months, and then change it back to your maiden name. If anyone asks, you are too grief-stricken to be reminded of the past. Better get it done before the baby is born, or you're going to have a constant reminder."

"As opposed to the baby being one?" Abby regretted the comment as soon as she said it. "I didn't mean that." Only a part of her did.

"Yes, you did, and it's perfectly understandable. But there's no need to worry. You will fall in love with her as soon as you hold her in your arms and kiss that sweet little face."

Abby frowned. "I wish I was as sure as you sound."

"I had a friend who was raped. She couldn't bring herself to terminate the pregnancy, nor did she want to raise the baby. She'd made all the preparations to give the child up for adoption and changed her mind the moment she heard him cry. And if for some reason you don't feel that way, then you'll give the little darling to me, and I'll raise her as my own."

"Thank you, Kevin."

"No, thank you," he said softly.

"For what?"

"For not saying no to that outright. Some would."

"I do love my baby. I am just overly hormonal and emotionally battered. I have no intention of giving my child up for adoption, but if I were not able to raise her, I would fully trust you to the task."

"And yet you barely know me."

"I know you have a good heart and that you put other's needs ahead of your own. I know that you shared your house with a psycho feline for days just to help me out, and that if I asked you to, you would get in the car right now to come save me. I know I don't have the best track record, but judging from your actions thus far, I know you will make a great father someday and that you will be a terrific auntie uncle to my daughter."

"When are you coming home?"

The comment caught her off guard. She faked a yawn. "I think I'm going to take a nap."

"Okay. Promise to call me if you need anything," Kevin replied. "Anytime, day or night."

"I promise," Abby said, disconnecting the call. She

Sinister Winds

placed the phone in her lap, staring at it as if it had just created the most heinous crime. Only it wasn't the phone who'd committed the act. It was Kevin. She'd never been in control of any aspect of her life, and now he'd just assumed she would follow him to Virginia. Running from one tragedy to what she'd considered a man who would keep her safe was precisely how she'd gotten into her current mess in the first place. But if not to Virginia, then where? She couldn't stay in New Orleans. Even if the house hadn't been destroyed, she would never feel safe living in Jacob's shadow. Plus, if Jacob was right about them coming for the baby, she needed to leave before giving birth. Kevin had suggested she go back to her maiden name, but even that life had been a lie.

Abby picked up the cup from the bedside table and drained the contents. Staring into space as the cold water slid down her throat, she pictured the newspaper clipping she'd found in Jacob's office that showed her birth parents, Todd and Clarice Rodgers, welcoming her home. Perhaps she could use their name. Then she thought of Brian, and her bottom lip trembled. Why couldn't he have been the father of her child?

"Damn you, Jacob Buckley. I hope you rot in your watery hell!" Abby said and flung the glass at the wall. The empty plastic cup did little to quell her anger. She picked up the plastic pitcher intending to throw it as well, when she heard a man's voice drifting into the room, mentioning her by name.

CHAPTER SEVEN

The door pushed open, and Abby sucked in her breath, letting it out slowly when she saw the man was wearing a white doctor's coat and had a stethoscope draped around his neck. A nurse she hadn't seen before followed him into the room and stood near the far wall.

The doctor smiled, his gleaming white teeth a bright contrast to his dark skin as he reached out his hand. "Mrs. Buckley, I'm Doctor Mark Putnam; I hear you've had quite the ordeal. How are you feeling?"

Abby shook his hand as her mind went through the list of emotions the comment provoked. Angry. Scared. Frustrated. Sad. Alone. She thought of the infant she now carried. No, not alone. "Better," she said, releasing his hand. Better than what, she hadn't a clue.

He nodded, then picked up her chart and leafed through it. "Good. You were severely dehydrated when they brought you in. So much so that when you complained about back pain, we worried about preterm labor. Given how early you are in your pregnancy, the baby would have little chance of survival, which is why we kept you. Your levels are much better. I think we are almost out of the woods, but I would like to keep you here a little longer so

Sinister Winds

we can continue giving you IV fluids just to be safe." He stepped up to the monitor and checked the readout. "I think we can remove the fetal monitor as well as the catheter and allow you to get out of bed on your own as long as you don't experience any more dizziness."

"I haven't noticed any more dizziness," Abby informed him.

"That could be because you haven't been out of bed. We'll see if it changes when we get you up and moving." He frowned at the chart, then let the papers fall into place. "I understand your husband didn't make it. Please accept my condolences. Have you spoken with anyone? I can have the chaplain come in to speak with you?"

She swallowed her unease. The last thing she needed was to share her murder confession with a priest. "No, thank you. I'm not Catholic."

"You don't have to be Catholic to speak to him. You seem to be in good spirits, but sometimes, it helps to talk to someone. I can have Social Services stop in."

"No, I am doing okay at the moment. I will schedule an appointment with my therapist when I get out." Abby resisted rolling her eyes when the doctor wrote something in her chart. *Great, now the man will think I'm unstable. Why, just because you killed your husband? And just like that, you're talking to yourself.* She coughed to cover a nervous giggle.

The doctor cocked his head but refrained from speaking as he sat the chart on the end of the bed and moved to listen to her heart and lungs. "Any complaints?"

Abby shook her head.

"Have you felt the baby kick?"

She smiled. "It's more like a flutter, but enough to let me know she's in there."

"And that's where we plan on keeping her. I know you have a lot on your mind right now, but do try to relax. You couldn't be in a safer place than where you are right now."

Safer? What was that supposed to mean? "Safe from what?"

He must have seen her frown as he held up a hand to ward off her worry. "I just meant that we are looking after you. You don't have to worry about finding a place to spend the night or anything else. You'll have enough to worry about once the baby is born."

If he only knew how accurate his words were.

He reached for the chart, jotted something on the paper, then turned to her once more. His eyes scanned her face and then trailed the length of her arms, coming to rest on the large knot on her forearm. He lifted his gaze and saw her watching him. "Those bruises on your face and arms, are they from the rescue?"

She started to tell him they were but didn't wish to get caught in a lie. "No."

"Your husband?" he asked.

"Was an evil man," Abby said softly.

He held her gaze. "You're safe here."

"Where is here?"

"Mississippi. The helicopter flew you here after you collapsed."

That she had no recollection of the second helo ride worried her. Still, it was a tad comforting to know she was further away from Jacob's reach, were he still alive. "As long as he is truly dead." *Shut up, Abby.*

"You think there is a possibility he is not?"

"No," she said truthfully. "But I guess until someone finds his body, I will always have a fear of him resurrecting."

Sinister Winds

"And, if he does, then what will you do?" the doctor inquired.

"About what?" Abby asked.

"Would you go with him?"

"He would not give me any other option."

"We all have a choice, Abigail."

With his smooth southern drawl, the man sounded so much like Jacob that the hairs on her arms stood on end. Thankfully, that was the only resemblance, so Abby was able to keep the tears at bay. "Not all of us," Abby said softly, struggling to control her voice. "You don't know my husband. If he were still alive, he would find me."

"You are safe here," the doctor repeated.

"Okay," Abby said. While she wanted to believe him, the instant he and the nurse left the room, tears sprang from her eyes.

***

Abby sat in the oversized chair with her legs pulled under her, staring out the window at the parking lot below. Though they'd removed the IV the day before, there'd been no mention of her being released from the hospital. Since she really had no place to go, she decided to remain quiet lest someone realize she no longer needed round-the-clock care. There was a knock at the door.

"Yes?" Abby said, turning from the window.

A man in a dark suit entered and stood just inside the door. He scanned the room before walking toward her and handing her a card.

She began to shake as she read it. Alfred Jefferies, FBI. Instantly, Abby knew why they'd been keeping her here; they'd found Jacob's body and were waiting for the FBI to arrest her. She recalled Gomez's advice and lowered her hand so he wouldn't see his presence frightened her. "What can I do for you, Mr. Jefferies?"

A perplexed scowl crossed his face. "To be honest, I haven't got a clue."

Okay, so not the answer she was expecting. "I'm afraid I don't understand."

"That makes two of us," he replied.

Something was off with the man. She'd watched enough television shows to know the FBI were competent or at least supposed to appear to be. This guy reminded her more of someone impersonating an agent than of someone in control of the situation. Abby glanced at the door, debating if she could make it into the hall before he caught her. Doubtful, since it would mean figuring out a way to distract him long enough for her to skirt around him. Okay, so perhaps she should offer him her chair. Once she sat on the bed, she could use the call button to summon help. "Here, take my chair," she said, untucking her legs.

"Don't get up. I'll sit over here." Jefferies walked to the edge of the wall and pulled a hard chair into the center of the room, blocking her way.

Shit. At least he left the door open. Now what? Maybe I should scream.

"I guess I should start at the beginning," Jefferies said after a long pause. "Doctor Putnam and I are old friends. He called me and told me about you and asked if I could come speak with you."

"So much for doctor-patient privilege," Abby said tersely.

Jefferies held up a hand to wave her off. "He didn't give me any particulars. Just told me you were afraid of your husband, who may or may not be alive."

"Okay, but why call the FBI? It's not as if I killed the man." *Shit, Abby, why'd you have to go and plant that seed?*

Jefferies arched an eyebrow. "No one is accusing you of anything and I am not here on official business."

Abby felt herself relax. "Well then, I'm afraid the good doctor is wasting your time. He asked if I wanted to speak to a chaplain or Social Services, and I told him no. I guess he forgot to ask if I wanted to speak to the FBI."

Apparently, Abby wasn't the only one feeling more relaxed as Jefferies sat back in the chair and crossed one leg over the other. He opened his mouth to say something, then closed it once more. "My friend told me you are afraid of your husband. Would you care to elaborate on why?"

"Nope. You said it yourself; you are not here on official business," she reminded him.

Jefferies' lip twitched. "What if I make it official?"

Abby tucked her hair behind her ear and adjusted her position in the chair. "Mr. Jefferies, I'm sorry Dr. Putnam made you come, but I've watched enough television to know that domestic violence does not warrant the FBI's attention."

Jefferies shifted in his chair. "I would have stopped in to see you a couple of days ago, but I was told they'd released you."

"Who told you they released me?"

"A nurse in the ER."

"Celie? You're the man in the suit." Abby groaned and clapped a hand over her mouth.

"Yes, she was rather adamant that you were released. Even went so far as to tell me she called you a cab," Jefferies said dryly.

"Is she in trouble?" Abby asked.

Jefferies uncrossed his leg and pulled the opposite leg across. "As I said, I am not here on official business."

Something about the man's story wasn't adding up. "You said you stopped by the ER a couple of days ago."

"That's right."

"You also said Dr. Putnam asked you to speak with me."

"Right again."

Abby leaned forward in her chair. "I did not see Dr. Putnam until yesterday. So, he couldn't have known about me before that."

Jefferies stared at her as if looking straight through her. Finally, he placed both feet on the floor and crossed his arms. "Mrs. Buckley, up until four days ago, I considered myself to be a perfectly sane individual. Since that time, I have had some experiences that have me questioning my sanity."

Abby looked at the door once more.

"I assure you; I am not here to hurt you."

"Then why are you here?"

"What can you tell me about a man by the name of Steven Merrick?" Jefferies asked.

That he's dead. Abby kept that tidbit to herself. The last thing she wanted was to get Kevin in trouble. "He was a business associate of my husband."

"What line of work was your husband in?"

"I do not know," Abby replied.

Jefferies cocked his head. "You were married to the man and never asked what he did for a living?"

Abby laughed. "Of course I did."

"He didn't tell you?"

"My husband was a very private man."

"What was your relationship with Merrick?"

"I had no relationship with the man."

"You were seen speaking with Merrick on more than

one occasion."

"I thought you said you're not here on official business. This sounds like an inquisition to me."

"It's neither." He smiled. "I could make it official if you'd prefer."

"He was my babysitter," Abby replied.

Jefferies stared at her. "Aren't you a bit old for a babysitter?"

"I'm also well past the age of being treated like a child and being punished for the least infraction. Unfortunately, my husband disagreed with me on that point."

Jefferies' eyes traced her bruises, and his face softened. He uncrossed his arms and crossed his legs once more. "Do you recall your whereabouts on April third of this year?"

"I could tell you every detail of that day."

"You must have a photographic memory."

"Far from it. April third was my wedding day, and what turned out to be the single worst day of my life, and I assure you, I've had some pretty bad days," she said, meeting his gaze.

"What time was the wedding?"

"It wasn't a wedding. Just a simple ceremony at a judge's house." She shrugged. "It was someone Jacob knew."

"The time?" Jefferies repeated.

"It was supposed to be one o'clock but didn't get started until twenty after."

"Merrick was there?"

"No, not for the ceremony. He showed up late. Jacob wasn't happy about it," she said, recalling her first time seeing the man. A shiver ran through her, remembering the reason for Merrick's delay. Hoping to discredit the man, she continued. "The ceremony was over at one thirty, and

Merrick came in a few minutes after it was over. The man looked as if he'd been in a fight. His clothes were torn and I'm pretty sure he had blood stains on his jacket. He signed the marriage certificate and left."

"And you are sure the man was Steven Merrick?"

She thought of the things she'd found in Jacob's office that revealed all the lies that surrounded her life. "Mr. Jefferies, at this point, I am not sure I'm the best judge of that. I know that is the name Jacob called him."

"Okay, let me reword the question. Is the man that followed you to the supermarket named Merrick?"

"Yes," Abby said softly.

"And he's the guy you call the babysitter who sits outside your house when your husband is away."

Abby frowned. "How do you know all of this?"

"It's my job." Jefferies uncrossed his legs, sat back in his chair once more and placed his palms together as if considering his next move. "Steven Merrick is a suspect in a murder investigation. The FBI has had a team following him for months, trying to catch him in the act."

Abby thought of Kevin, and her heart sank. If the FBI had been following Merrick, they may not have seen Kevin drag the man from the house, but they must have seen him dispose of the car. She worked to keep her voice even. "You've been following the man?"

Jefferies nodded. "Up until about a week ago. The agency decided to pull the team right before the hurricane arrived."

Oh, thank God. That means Kevin is safe. Abby emitted a nervous giggle.

Jefferies raised an eyebrow. "Did I say something funny?"

Abby shook her head. "No."

"Then why were you laughing?"

"It just dawned on me that if you were better at your job, you would have caught him earlier, and maybe my life would have turned out differently."

"Different, how?"

"I hate to break it to you, Mr. Jefferies, but you've had your team following the wrong monster. Merrick may have killed Eva Radoux, but my husband is the one who unleashed the dog."

"The dog being Merrick?"

Abby nodded.

Jefferies' mouth twitched. "You'd testify to that?"

"I thought your visit was unofficial."

He shrugged. "It just got official."

"Mr. Jefferies, before we go on the record, I would like to ask you a question."

Jefferies nodded. "Go on."

"When you came into the room, you seemed like a different man and went so far as to question your sanity. Nothing we have discussed here today warrants that, so what had you upset?"

"Did you know Eva Radoux?"

"Are we still off the record?"

"For now," Jefferies replied.

"No, I didn't know her."

"Are you sure? Because we have a witness that saw a redhead that matches your description speaking with her the day before her death."

Tread carefully, Abby warned herself. "I did speak with her, but I didn't know her."

"But she knows you?"

There was something about the way he asked the question. An urgency, perhaps, that gave her pause.

Though he knew Eva to be dead, he framed the question in the present tense. He was in the hospital even before the doctor told him about her. Abby smiled. "She came to you in a dream."

Jefferies' eyes grew wide. "How did you know?"

Abby relaxed for the first time since the man had entered the room. Eva wouldn't have sent him unless she knew she could trust him. "Because you're not the only one. It's why Celie told you I'd been sent home. Eva came to her in a dream and told her to protect me."

"From me?"

"No," Abby said, believing it to be true. "Not if she sent you here."

"The thing I don't understand," Jefferies said as he ran his hands through his hair, "is how any of this is even possible. I'm an educated man and not someone who believes in hocus pocus. I know everything that has transpired over the past week is impossible, and yet, here I am."

"I'd tell you I had all the answers," Abby replied. "But I'm afraid that isn't the case."

"I guess we should get back to the record. You'll excuse me if I skirt around the dream aspect of the case."

"I think that may be for the best," Abby agreed.

"Do you need anything before we begin?"

"I could really go for a chocolate shake, a taco, and a slice of pizza," Abby said, and her mouth watered.

He stood.

"Seriously?" Abby asked.

"As long as you promise to be here when I return," Jefferies said firmly.

"Mr. Jefferies, it wouldn't do any good for me to run. They always know where to find me."

Sinister Winds

He stopped just inside the door. "They?"

"Oh, you don't know? Eva has a sister, and they seem to work as a team." Abby smiled. Up until that moment, she had never seen anyone turn that white.

CHAPTER EIGHT

Abby paced the floor, waiting for Jefferies to return. She debated calling Kevin but knew he would only bombard her with questions she couldn't answer and insist she ask for an attorney, who would likely tell her to remain silent. Knowing Eva sent the man gave her comfort and added to her anxiety all at the same time. Why would she send him if she were no longer in danger? Though she didn't look forward to reliving the past, she hoped that doing so would help them both find the answers they were seeking and somehow lead to a way of keeping her child safe.

"Knock knock. I would have used my hand, but they are both full," Jefferies said as he came into the room carrying multiple bags and a whole pizza box, plus a cardboard carrier with two drinks, all of which he placed on the small round table that sat between two chairs near the window.

"Holy smoke," Abby said, eyeing the bounty. "I hope you don't expect me to eat all of this."

Jefferies reached into the bag, pulled out a package of paper plates, and handed her one. "If my sister is any indication of what a pregnant woman can eat, you'll eat all

Sinister Winds

of this and then some. But to help you save face, I'll help you down some of it while we chat. Don't worry; I cleared it with your doctor, who assures me you're not on a restricted diet."

Abby reached into the box and pulled out a slice of pizza. She giggled her delight as most of the cheese from an adjoining slice broke free and landed on top of the slice.

Jefferies eyed the box. "You're not going to put that back, are you?"

"What is it they say about possession being nine-tenths of the law?" Abby said, biting into the slice.

"You're pretty smart, Mrs. Buckley. So I have to ask how it is you ended up with a man who used you like a punching bag?"

"Wow, you don't pull any punches, do you?" Abby shrugged off the comment. "I mean…"

"I know what you meant, and being direct is normally one of my virtues except when dealing with things I cannot explain. So, I'll ask you again, what attracted you to the man?"

"Do you want the long version of the story or the one I told myself?" Abby took a bite of pizza and waited for his answer.

"Perhaps you should start at the beginning," Jefferies replied.

"I was born in California."

"Okay, maybe not that far back." Jefferies chuckled.

"Oh, but that is the beginning. I was not aware of it until a few days ago. It is a fascinating story, Mr. Jefferies. I'm sure it would make an intriguing movie of the week."

He lifted a slice of pizza from the box. "I'm listening."

"Jacob, that's my husband, was in love with my mother, and thought her to be in love with him as well right up until she married someone else. My mom got pregnant right away, and apparently, I was a carbon copy of the woman. Still furious by the rejection, Jacob saw this as the perfect opportunity to exact his revenge. He burned our house, rescued me, and placed me with another family in Indiana."

"You didn't realize your parents weren't your parents?" Jefferies asked.

"Old memories fade over time. When I think of the fire, I recall being scared, but anytime it was brought up, my parents would praise Jacob for his heroics." She wiped at a tear. "They would tell me how lucky we were to have him in our lives and how, if it weren't for Jacob, I wouldn't be there with them."

Jefferies handed her a napkin. "And what, you just remembered all of it?"

"No, shortly after our wedding, it became apparent Jacob was hiding something. That thought was confirmed when Pearl told me I couldn't leave until I knew the truth. So, I waited until he was gone and snooped," she said, omitting Kevin's part for the moment. "I found the newspaper articles and my birth certificate hidden behind a false wall in the desk."

"And you hadn't seen these things before?"

"Jacob kept his office locked and forbade me to go in there."

"I don't assume you managed to bring the documents you found with you?"

"No, but the authorities knew I was missing. There were newspaper articles, rewards, and everything. You're the FBI; my birth name was Clarissa Rodgers, and my birth parents' names were Todd and Clarice Rodgers. I'm sure you can verify my story. I mean, don't you have a database for this stuff?"

"We'll find it," Jefferies said, jotting in his notebook. "Please continue with your story."

"As I said, Jacob was a friend of the family, always coming around and bringing me gifts."

"How convenient," Jefferies muttered.

"Yes, well. I didn't think a lot of it. I mean, I liked him, but that's because he was always nice to me, and who doesn't like presents? Then, when I grew older, my dad started talking him up and saying what a good guy Jacob was and how maybe I should consider marrying him."

"Your dad didn't have a problem with the age difference?"

She stopped chewing and looked him in the eyes. "Jacob paid my parents to groom me for him."

"What a sick son of a ..." Jefferies held up his hands. "Sorry."

"No, you're right. I think Mom realized it at some point because she quit talking him up. She was thrilled when I met Brian." Abby saw the question in Jefferies's eyes and continued. "Brian was everything Jacob wasn't. He was loud, spontaneous, and had a playful sense of humor. I guess he was a bit of a bad boy, and to be honest, that was what I loved about him." She rubbed her hands along her arms. "I can still recall Jacob's face when I told him. He was furious. So was Dad. He said I'd ruined everything. They both ganged up on me and tried to pressure us into getting an annulment. But Brian wouldn't hear of it."

"Where is this Brian now?"

"Dead. Jacob killed him."

"You knew this and still married the man?"

"I came home from work expecting to find Brian asleep because he'd worked the night shift. Instead, I found him sitting in the recliner." She blew out a breath to steady herself. "I didn't even know he did drugs, then to find him with a needle in his arm and foaming at the mouth... My dad started talking up Jacob once more, but my mom seemed different. Looking back, I think she was scared."

"Did you ask her about it?"

Abby sighed. "I didn't have a chance. I was a mess after Brian died, and it seemed as if my dad never wanted me to talk to her alone. My parents had died from carbon monoxide poisoning a couple of months later, and sure enough, Jacob was there to pick up the pieces. He was so kind and helped me wade through the paperwork. He convinced me to go back to my maiden name, Turner, and wanted me to move to New Orleans with him. It was too soon. I just needed time to think. However, the apartment had too many memories, and Jacob was persistent. By the time it was time to renew the lease on my apartment, he'd convinced me that my only chance of happiness was with him." She laughed to keep from crying again. "I second-guessed myself the whole drive down here. I can't tell you how many times I considered turning around."

"Why didn't you?"

"Because when I ran through everything bad that had ever happened in my life, the one consistent person was Jacob. He was the only thing solid, the only person who'd always been there, and he made me feel safe." She was trembling and worked to keep the anger from overcoming her.

"When did that change?"

"The day I married him, but I'll get to that in a minute."

"Okay, take your time," Jefferies said softly.

"I came to New Orleans with everything I had left stuffed into my car. I also had Ned, my Quaker parrot, and

Gulliver, my cat. Jacob hated animals, but I'd told him it was a package deal. He agreed, saying it was worth the price to have me. I bought his lies, and because of him, Ned is dead. Can you believe it, he killed my freaking bird? He blamed it on the cat, but Gulliver would never have hurt Ned." She sniffed, remembering. "Sorry, I really loved that bird. He didn't have to kill him. He could have just opened the door and let him fly away. How could a man who proclaimed to love me want to hurt me that way?"

"Did he kill the cat too?"

Abby sniffed and shook her head. "No, Kevin took him to Virginia when he left. He wanted me to come too, but Pearl told me I couldn't go." She held up a hand to ward off his questions. "I'll get there."

Jefferies remained silent.

"There were red flags, but Jacob was good at explaining everything away. He was short with me a couple of times when I pressed the issue, like why I wasn't allowed in his office or why he didn't trust me enough not to lock the door. But he didn't raise a hand to me—not yet, anyway. We lived together for a few months and never shared anything more than a kiss. Oh, I tried, but Jacob refused. He was old-fashioned that way—at least that was what he told me. It was endearing in a way, that he respected me so much. I didn't so much as leave the yard for the first couple of months. I didn't mind all that much; I was still in mourning and it didn't dawn on me to care. Then one day, Jacob came in and told me we were going to town. It was such a lovely day. We walked through the French Quarter with Jacob showing me the sights. I was having a grand old time and then someone stole my purse. Jacob ran after the guy and told me to stay there. But then he didn't come back right away. I got scared and went after him. That's when I met Eva."

Jefferies frowned. "You said you didn't know her."

"I didn't, not in the way your question implied. I went after Jacob to make sure he was okay. I got turned around and started to panic because I had no clue what I was supposed to do if he never returned. All of a sudden, Eva was there."

"You're saying she just appeared out of nowhere?"

"I don't know. I hadn't seen her before and then she was standing in the doorway. She called me over, and my feet started moving. She took hold of my hand." Tears started to flow once more. "She tried to warn me, but I was scared. Then she started speaking in French and spat on the ground. I don't speak French, but I guess she scared me enough that I remembered her words. *Il est le fils du diable.* She followed it up with *L'homme a un coeur noir.* She was so angry. She terrified me. I ran, and when I reached the street, Jacob was there. He was scared, and I was scared. I repeated what the woman said, saying it in French the best I could. He told me…"

"She told you *he was the son of the Devil and you were marrying a man with a black heart,*" Jefferies said, cutting her off.

"I could have used you a few months ago," Abby replied. "Only that is not the way Jacob interpreted it. He told me she'd said I was marrying an old man. Anyway, the whole purse snatch thing was a setup. By taking away my purse and keys, Jacob managed to break down the last of my defenses. That night, I agreed to marry Jacob, and by the next day, he'd arranged everything. I found it, you know."

"Found what?"

"My purse. It was in the cabinet with everything else.

Another reminder that the man who I thought was there to protect me had orchestrated every detail and was controlling my whole life."

"When did the abuse start?"

"On our wedding day." Abby laughed, though nothing about the situation was funny. "I was his property, and he had the paper to prove it."

"Why didn't you leave?"

"I told him I was going to. He reminded me that I had nowhere else to go. He'd taken everything. I had no identification, no money, no car keys. The next day, it was as if nothing had happened, and I found myself wondering what I'd done to provoke him. I was feeling off and thought it was from the beating. But when he beat me again, I threatened to go to the police."

"What'd he say?"

"He told me he had friends in high places and that I had enough drugs in my system to have me locked away. So I stayed, and you pretty much know the rest."

Jefferies' nostrils flared, then recovered. "So what you're telling me is Eva Radoux was killed for trying to warn you about Jacob?"

"Yes."

"Then why is she trying to protect you?"

"I asked Pearl the same thing."

"Pearl? That's the sister you spoke of?"

Abby nodded.

"How did you two meet?"

"She found me in the cereal aisle of the grocery store and introduced herself." She noticed his frown and started from the beginning. "I convinced Jacob to allow me to go to the grocery store. I was walking through the aisles, making plans to leave him, and then Pearl showed up."

"What did she say?"

"She said Eva and she were the same and that they talked in the dream world. They are voodoo priestesses."

"So I've heard." Jefferies' voice held doubt.

She continued without trying to convince him. "She said Eva knew it wasn't my fault, and she gave me a pouch for protection."

"Pouch?"

Abby debated for a moment before showing him the small leather pouch she'd hidden behind her in the chair. She handed it to him and watched as he opened the bag.

His eyes grew wide. Then he closed the bag without touching its contents. "I've heard a chicken foot holds powerful magic," he said, returning the bag.

"That's what my neighbor said."

"Your neighbor. That would be one Kevin Bishop?"

Abby closed her eyes briefly. She'd hoped to keep Kevin out of the conversation. "Yes."

"What is your relationship with Mr. Bishop?"

Abby smiled. "He is a friend."

"How good of a friend?"

"We are not having an affair, if that is what you are asking."

"I didn't say that."

"You implied it. No, Mr. Jefferies, Kevin and I are not having an affair. Kevin is a friend and nothing more."

"You said earlier that he asked you to come with him."

She took her time debating her answer. Finally, she decided to tell him the truth. "Yes, when he was, what do they call it, bugging out? He took Gulliver to keep him safe, but I refused to go."

"How come?"

She started to tell him that Pearl told her not to but

decided against it. "Because everyone I come in contact with ends up dead."

"You said you were going to leave. What changed your mind?" Jefferies asked, circling back.

"I spent too much time talking to Pearl, then I was talking to Kevin."

"So this Kevin guy just happens to show up in the store at the same time you were thinking about leaving your husband? Are you sure the two of you hadn't planned this all along?"

Abby recalled the first real conversation she'd had with Kevin and laughed.

"Care to share what you find so amusing?"

"The grocery was the closest to Dumas Street. Before that day, Kevin and I'd spoken briefly in the yard, and I assure you neither of us enjoyed the conversation. Nor did we hit it off. He thought I was a dumbass for being with Jacob, and I thought he was a pompous bitch." Abby shrugged. "I'd taken some rosemary from his bush, and he called me on it."

"Rosemary?"

"The plant."

"I know what rosemary is, Mrs. Buckley."

"He and Jacob had had words before, and Kevin didn't like the fact I was associated with him."

"What kind of words?"

"My husband didn't like his kind."

Jefferies arched his brow. "His kind?"

"Kevin Bishop is gay, Mr. Jefferies. Yes, I love him. He has been there for me ever since he found out that Jacob was abusing me. I consider him a dear friend, but we are not, nor will we ever be, romantically involved."

Jefferies shook his head in subtle understanding. "That

day in the grocery, why didn't you leave?"

"Jacob called. He wanted to know why I was taking so long in the store and told me he and Gulliver were having a nice time together. I knew if I didn't go home, he would kill him. Then, when I came out of the store, Merrick was in the lot waiting for me. It drove home the point that Jacob wasn't ever going to let me leave."

"Did you ever see Pearl again?"

"Yes, she showed up several times over the course of the next few months. Always with a warning or instructions." *No trust stranger.* Abby recalled a conversation with Celie while in the ER. The nurse had told her Eva had visited her in her dreams and told her the same thing. She swallowed and looked at the man sitting before her. What if he wasn't who he said he was? He hadn't actually shown her a badge, and how hard was it to print up a card? She reached her hands to her temples. "Mr. Jefferies, I'm suddenly feeling unwell. Would it be all right if we continue this conversation another time?"

Jefferies rose from his chair. He looked from her to the door. "Should I call the nurse?"

"No," she said, shaking her head. "It's just a headache. I'll be okay if I lie down for a while."

"Of course. I'll come back and check on you later."

"Can we make it tomorrow? Sometimes, these migraines take all day to go away."

He frowned. "Okay, I'll stop in tomorrow."

"I'll be here," she said, knowing it was a lie.

CHAPTER NINE

Abby waited until she was sure Jefferies was gone before dialing Kevin's number. "Kevin, he was here!" she sobbed into the phone the second he answered.

Kevin's gasp was audible. "The Dick is still alive? Where are you?"

"No...Mississippi. It wasn't him. I'm still in the hospital, and the man came to see me. He says he's with the FBI."

"Wait. What do you mean, he says he's with the FBI? Don't you believe him?"

"I'm not the best judge of people."

"That's true."

"You don't have to agree with me."

"Sunshine, you know I'd never lie to you. Now tell me what happened and how the FBI got involved."

"He came to my hospital room and started asking all these questions."

"And you answered his questions?"

"He brought food. It's not funny," Abby said when Kevin's laughter floated through the phone. "I'm pregnant and was craving pizza and a milkshake. He wanted to know everything. At first, he said it was off the record, but then when I told him about Jacob, he said we should probably make it official."

"If the Dick is dead, why is he interested in him?"

"He wasn't at first. He came here asking about Merrick."

Another gasp. "They found his body?"

"Not yet. But they know he killed Eva. At least, they thought he did. They just couldn't prove it until I told him that Jacob ordered Merrick to do it."

"Did you ever think to ask for an attorney?" Kevin groaned.

"I figured if they knew about Jacob, they would concentrate on him. Mr. Jefferies, that's the guy's name, said they had Merrick under surveillance until right before the hurricane. Thank goodness they made them leave ahead of the storm. It sucks. They were so intent on nailing Merrick, yet they never once thought of checking out the man he was working for. I guess that shows how thorough Jacob was. But at least they stopped the surveillance before…"

"What happened to not talking about things on the phone?" Kevin asked, cutting her off.

Shit. She'd been so upset that she'd totally forgotten about that. "I'm sorry. I should let you go."

"No, it's okay, Sunshine. We have nothing to hide."

Though he'd said it in a convincing manner, Abby knew he was worried. "I spilled almost everything, and then he asked about Pearl. I knew it would lead to things better left unsaid, so I feigned a headache and…"

"Not for nothing, but you're giving me a headache," Kevin said, cutting her off. "If you didn't trust the man, why would you even talk to him? I'm sorry to be so frank, but seriously, Abby, it's almost like you want to be caught."

"Huh."

"Huh, what?" Kevin asked.

"Nothing. I just don't think you've ever used my name before."

"Are you on drugs? I hope the answer's yes, because if you are, then nothing you've said is admissible in court."

"I'm not on drugs, and I've not said anything to implicate either one of us. I don't have any reason not to tell him about Pearl either. It's just when he asked about her, I remembered Pearl saying not to trust strangers. But if Eva sent him, then maybe she thinks he can be trusted. I mean, why else would she send him?"

Kevin's voice rose a full decibel. "He told you the voodoo princess sent him?"

"Yes, she visited him in his dream. Didn't I say that?"

"No, you didn't say it. If you had, we could have skipped over this whole conversation. Everything Pearl has told you up until now has kept you safe. Why would you think it would change now that the Dick is dead? She must know you're still in danger, which is why she sent the FBI. It's pretty cool, by the way."

"What is?"

"That a dead Cajun woman can tap into the dream world and call in the cavalry."

"Yeah, pretty cool."

"You don't sound convinced," Kevin replied. "You don't think it's amazing?"

"I guess. But why the dance?"

"The dance?"

"Yeah, it just feels like a bunch of hocus pocus. If she can reach the FBI, then why not do it in the first place? You know, just plug into the guy's head and say, you don't know me, but I'm dead, and this is the guy who killed me."

"I don't know. Maybe she didn't think the guy would believe her," Kevin suggested.

"He doesn't."

"He told you that?"

"Not in those exact words, but I can see it on his face. The visit from Eva scared him."

"Good!" Kevin said.

"Why good?"

"Because if he were lying, he'd have no reason to be scared. I still remember your face that day you first met Pearl. You were flabbergasted."

Okay, Kevin had a point. "Are you saying I should talk to him about Pearl?"

"Only if you want, but it couldn't hurt as long as you don't admit to murder."

"I didn't kill anyone."

Kevin laughed. "Now say it like you mean it."

"Okay, but I don't want to tell him about the baby."

More laughter. "If he's seen you, then I'm pretty sure he knows you're pregnant."

"No, I mean about Jacob selling our unborn child." Just saying it out loud caused her heart to clench.

"Why?"

Such a simple question to which she had no answer. "I don't know."

"Maybe it's your motherly instincts," Kevin offered.

Abby sighed. "I'm not even sure if I have those."

"Sure you do, Sugar."

"Kevin?"

"Yes?"

"I think I prefer it when you call me Sunshine. Hey," she said before he could respond. "Thanks for talking me down. I'm feeling much better about staying and talking to the guy."

"Are you sure you're okay? I can still come be with you."

"No, I promise I'm good."

"Okay, but just know if you need me, even if it is just to hold your hand. I'll come."

"Thank you, Kevin. I'll call you after I talk to him tomorrow. Give Gulliver a kiss for me."

"Will do, Sunshine. You take care of my niece and tell her Uncle Kevin can't wait to meet her."

"I will," Abby said and disconnected the call. She put the phone on the table, sat in the chair, and pulled her knees as far to her chest as possible. Though Kevin's energy was anything but calm, talking with him made her feel better. Though she'd only known the guy a short time, she realized she was closer and more comfortable with him than she'd ever been with Jacob. She chided herself for her earlier fear of joining Kevin in Virginia. It wasn't as if he were asking for anything other than offering to be her friend. Except for the child she was carrying, she was alone in the world, and if anything happened to her, the baby would be alone as well. She picked up the cell phone and pulled up Kevin's name once more and typed in a message. >*Thank you for everything. You're a great guy and are going to be a wonderful uncle to my baby.* She hit send and waited for a reply. She didn't have to wait long.

Kevin > *I know.*

Abby reached and placed the phone on the table beside her. As she stretched, she felt the baby move. Instead of the previous subtle flutter of movement, this was a defined kick. She rubbed at the spot where she felt the kick and smiled. She then managed a nearly perfect imitation of Kevin's voice. "That's it, Sugar, kick those legs and show

Momma what you've got."

***

Freshly showered, Abby pulled on the hospital gown and somehow managed to tie it before pulling on a second one to use as a robe. She slipped into the sandals Celie had sent her and had just returned to the outer room when she heard a knock on the door. "Yes?"

The door pushed open, and Alfred Jefferies stepped into the room, holding a white paper bag and a paper cup.

"Good thing I'm an early riser," Abby said, sliding a glance at the clock on the wall, which showed it to be seven a.m.

Jefferies held up the bag. "I brought donuts."

Abby narrowed her eyes. "Just because I'm pregnant doesn't mean I'm weak when it comes to food. The doctor hasn't even been in yet; you should come back at a respectable time."

He smiled and offered her the cup he was holding. "And a milkshake."

Her mouth watered as she took the offering along with a straw he pulled from his shirt pocket. "Where on earth did you get a milkshake at this hour of the morning?"

"At the getting place." He winked. "My mother used to tell me that whenever I asked an unnecessary question. Does that mean I can stay?"

She shrugged as she backed into the oversized chair. "I guess, since you're already here. Do you always interrogate people this early?" she asked and reached for the bag.

"It's not an interrogation. And only if I suspect the person I'm going to speak with is a flight risk. To be honest, I'm a bit surprised you're still here," he said, then pulled a donut from the bag and took a bite. "You looked a bit unsettled when I left yesterday."

"And if I had left?"

"You wouldn't have gotten very far." He shrugged. "I had a member of my team watching the exit to this wing."

Abby recalled Kevin's words. "Is this where I ask for an attorney?"

Jefferies leaned back in his chair. "Do you feel you need one?"

"Let me ask you this, Mr. Jefferies. If I was your sister, would you advise me to call an attorney?" A smile pulled at the man's lips, and Abby found herself wondering at what was rolling through the man's mind as he silently pulled a tissue from the box and wiped his hands.

"I plan on having a long and productive career with the agency. I'd rather them not be privy to what we discuss today. So, no, I wouldn't wish for anything we discuss to be on the record," he said at last. "If we get to a place where that changes, or where I would advise my own sister to ask for an attorney, I will let you know."

Abby nodded her agreement. "What is it you wish to know, Mr. Jefferies?"

Jefferies ran a hand through his hair. "I want to know how it is possible for a dead woman to visit me in my dreams. A dream, I get, but this was more. The woman is dead. I've personally seen the body. How is an educated man such as myself supposed to make sense of this?"

Abby struggled to keep from laughing. "Mr. Jefferies, if that is why you came here, I'm afraid you're wasting your time. I don't have those answers."

"No, I didn't think you would. But I figured it was worth asking. So how about we try and figure this thing out together, shall we?"

"I suppose we can try."

Jefferies pulled a small black notebook from his pocket. "Okay, I'll start by telling you what I know so far, which is really just confirming what you've already told me. I did a search on Todd and Clarice Rodgers and confirmed their deaths in the fire and a nationwide search for the child, who was never found. I'm certain you are the child in question and probably have family out there somewhere."

Abby felt her pulse quicken. "No."

"No?" Jefferies said, parroting her words.

"I've seen how all this works. I would be on the cover of every tabloid in the country. I'd be like the little girl who fell down the well; neither I nor my baby would know a moment's peace."

"What about any family you might have out there?"

She hadn't thought of that. No, it didn't matter. What did matter was keeping her baby safe from those who would come for her. "My family is dead," Abby said firmly.

Jefferies patted the air with his hands. "Calm down. We can hash this all out later. Now, on to Marsha and Brad Turner. Marsha had a clean record, and Brad had some petty offenses back in the day. It looks like he cleaned his act up around the same time you went to live with them. I'd like to tell you he changed his ways, but if your husband did the things you say, then him staying out of the public eye was probably part of the deal."

"Brad liked his beer and his video games. He wasn't a bad father, mostly because I rarely spent any time alone with him. I mean he was there, but it wasn't as if we did anything together. I used to ask Mom what she saw in him, but she'd just smile and say that I was here because of him. I used to think she meant that in the normal way a man and woman have a child. Boy, was I wrong." Abby rubbed at the goose bumps that appeared on her arms. "I guess I should be grateful the guy wasn't a pervert."

Jefferies nodded his agreement. "Brian's death was ruled an overdose, but you already know that. I could ask them to reopen the case and cite new evidence, but if you're sure your husband killed him, there's no reason to do that unless the man turns up alive."

"That means I'll have to testify?"

"Only if your husband is alive."

"I hate that his family thinks he did that to himself."

"Take heed, Mrs. Buckley. I'll put a guy on it and see if we can find a way to clear your ex-husband's name," Jefferies said and jotted something on the notebook.

"Now, if you can find a way to clear my name," Abby said softly.

"Your name?"

"Every time you call me Mrs. Buckley, I feel as if I will throw up. I don't think I could stomach giving my child her father's name."

"You hate the man that much?"

"More than you'll ever know," Abby replied.

Jefferies jotted in the notebook once more. "I'm pretty sure we can also connect your adoptive parents' deaths to Jacob as well."

"I agree," Abby said, knowing it was true.

"Tell me about Pearl," Jefferies said.

"I don't know anything about her other than she told me she's Eva's sister."

"How many times have you spoken with her?"

"Four."

"Where did you meet?"

"You say that as if they were scheduled."

"They weren't?"

Abby shook her head. "No, she just showed up."

"Where?"

"In the grocery store mainly."

"You're saying she just showed up?"

Abby nodded.

"Four times without you telling her you were going to be there?"

"No."

"So, you did tell her."

"I meant not all were at the grocery store. One time, she found me when Jacob took me to the post office with him."

A sly smile crossed Jefferies' face. "Have you ever thought that your meeting with the woman might have been a ruse?"

"I'm not following you," Abby replied.

"Your husband knew you were going to the store. Do you think perhaps this woman wasn't who she said she was and that he was putting her up to contacting you?"

"Not possible."

"Why not?"

"Because she knew what Eva and I discussed."

"Which you repeated to your husband," Jefferies reminded her.

"I did. But she also knew what Merrick told her sister before he killed her."

"Which she would have known if either your husband or Merrick told her."

While true, Abby didn't believe it to be. "She also gave me the charm for protection."

"That would be the chicken foot you showed me."

"Yes. Jacob would not have agreed to it." She held up a finger to show she wasn't finished. "Mr. Jefferies, my husband was a vile and evil man who enjoyed punishing me. If he had known about the charm, he would have made it his mission to find it and would have taken immense pleasure in punishing me for having it. No, you are not going to convince me he knew about that."

"Perhaps she thought of it on her own to add to the charade."

"I assure you Jacob would have been precise in his orders and would have also been precise in letting her know the consequences of them not being followed to the letter."

"Okay, so Pearl just happens to know you are at the store. She gives you the pouch. Then what?"

"Not quite. She comes up to me and tells me Eva came to her in a dream and that Eva knows Jacob sent the man to kill her. She said Eva wasn't happy that I didn't listen to her warning. I told her I didn't speak French and that is why I didn't listen. That's when she told me Eva said I need protection, and so she gave me the chicken foot."

"Then what?"

"She left, and before I could look to see where she was going, Kevin showed up."

"Okay, we've been through that. So when is the next time you met her?"

"A month and a half later, in the same store. Jacob had pushed me into the counter, and I'd hit my back. Pearl showed up. She seemed sad and touched my back exactly where the pain was. Her touch took my pain away. She must have known I was almost to the end of my rope because she told me not to leave."

"Pretty convenient."

"She told me I was pregnant and gave me a tea to help with the morning sickness to keep Jacob from learning I was pregnant."

"You didn't know you were pregnant?"

"No, I thought I was just sick of being used as Jacob's punching bag."

"Did she say anything else?"

Abby debated her answer for several moments. "She told me I couldn't leave without knowing the truth and not to trust the stranger."

"Did you know who she was speaking of?"

"Jacob invited a friend over, and I was at the store getting stuff to prepare a meal. Before you ask, I did not know the man."

"Was it normal for your husband to bring in guests?"

"No. This was a first. Jacob was acting strange before I left. When I returned home, I discovered the reason why. While I was gone, he killed my bird and blamed it on my cat."

"You're sure the cat didn't…"

"I already told you, Gulliver and Ned were friends. I have left them in the same room together, uncaged, many times. Jacob hated both the bird and the cat. I knew if he killed the bird, it would only be a matter of time before he killed my cat, so that's why I asked Kevin to take him when he left."

"This friend, did he have a name?"

"Nathan Riggs."

Jefferies wrote the name in his book. "Anything else you can tell me about the man?"

"Tall, handsome, and outgoing. From the way he dressed to the way he spoke, he reminded me of a surfer. He was much younger than my husband, and nothing about him gave any hint as to why he and Jacob were friends."

"Do you recall what they talked about?"

Bile rose in Abby's throat. "The man was a relentless flirt all through dinner and Jacob just sat there allowing it."

"That doesn't make sense."

"Not at the time. But after dinner Nathan made his move, and I was so ready to allow him to take me away until I remembered Pearl's words, no trust stranger, so I told him I was loyal to my husband."

"What'd he do?"

"He laughed, Mr. Jefferies! It was all a big game to test my loyalty. Nathan was still laughing when Jacob came into the room, beaming his delight that I'd passed the test. A test! Don't you see, if Pearl hadn't warned me, Jacob would have probably killed me?"

"You seem certain of that."

Abby blew out a long breath to steady herself. "I knew how close I'd come to saying yes, and I got mad and yelled at them. Jacob didn't like that I'd acted out in front of his friend and followed me into the bedroom. He used my outburst to teach me another of his lessons, and having an audience listening in from the other side of the door spurred him on." A wave of nausea washed over her as she recalled what he had done to her. That beating, coupled with listening to the two men talk and laugh into the night, was too much. She pushed from the chair, hurried to the bathroom, and emptied the contents of her stomach.

CHAPTER TEN

Abby stayed in the bathroom so long that she half expected Jefferies to tire of waiting and leave. Unfortunately, the man was tenacious in his quest for knowledge and was waiting for her when she returned to the room. To his credit, the guy's face was creased with concern when he stood and waited for her to return to her chair.

"Are you okay?" he asked, hovering over her.

Abby waved him off. "Better. Thank you."

"Mrs. Buckley, I don't pretend to know what went on in that house, but I promise you that I will do everything in my power to keep you and the little one safe."

While Abby wanted to believe him, Pearl's words kept her from fully trusting the man. If Jacob had enough power to control a judge, surely he would be able to influence someone in the FBI. "Ask your questions, Mr. Jefferies."

"What happened next?"

"I was worried about the baby, so I pretended Jacob had beaten me into submission."

"When did you next see Pearl?" Jefferies asked.

"At the post office. Jacob had to mail an envelope and insisted I go with him."

"Was it normal for him to invite you along?"

"Only when Merrick wasn't available."

"Maybe we could verify Merrick's whereabouts. Do you recall the date?"

"No."

"What about the envelope? Did you happen to see the address?"

"No. Whatever it was, it was important because he insisted on taking it inside himself."

"He wasn't worried about you driving off?"

"He must have been, as he took the keys with him." She smirked. "At least he had the decency to roll the windows down."

"That was nice of him. You must have known Merrick wasn't around. How come you didn't leave?"

"I thought about it. I figured I could tell someone what was going on, and they'd give me a ride."

Jefferies raised a brow. "What stopped you?"

"Pearl. A pregnant woman came out, and I'd made up my mind to ask her for help when Pearl appeared beside my car and told me she'd had a vision of what Jacob would do to her when he found her."

"And, of course, you believed her." Though he was smiling, his tone was condescending.

Abby stared into his eyes as she answered. "Mr. Jefferies. At this point in my life, there are two people who have not let me down. One is Kevin Bishop, and the other is Pearl Duval." She wanted to count Brian in the mix, but she was still angry with the man for dying.

"Noted. Please continue."

"Pearl told me I couldn't leave until I knew the truth. Kevin and I had already discussed that. I told Kevin that Jacob kept his key on his keyring, and he suggested there was another key. I'd been looking everywhere but had yet to find it. Pearl pointed to the console and told me the key was in there."

Jefferies looked up from his notes. "She actually told you that?"

"I believe her exact words were 'what you seek is in there.' She was right: the key was in there."

"You weren't afraid of getting caught with it?"

"Terrified. I was able to get the key to Kevin, who made a copy so I could return it before Jacob noticed it was missing."

"Your neighbor…"

"Is a wonderful human being who was trying to help me out of a terrible situation," Abby said, cutting him off. "He risked his life more than once, and I'll not have you accuse him of any ill proprieties."

"Sounds like a good friend," Jefferies replied. "So Pearl told you to stay, and you had the key. Now what?"

She thought about telling him about the spell Pearl put on Jacob so he would chill out, but the man was already skeptical, so she pressed on. "Having the key and being able to find the opportunity to use it were two separate things. Jacob went for weeks without leaving the house, and when he did, he made me go with him. He was better for a while, only hitting me when I overstepped, which I tried not to do." She showed him the knot on her arm. "Sometimes, I couldn't help myself."

"Have you had it looked at?"

"No, Jacob wasn't much for doctors. I figure it's too late to do anything about it now."

"He didn't believe in medical treatment?"

"It wasn't that. I think he was afraid I'd spill my guts if I was in the room alone with someone who might be able to help me. That's why he insisted on going to my OB appointments with me."

"Was he happy about the baby?"

"He couldn't have been happier," Abby said without explaining the reason why.

"And you?"

"I was in shock at first, then afraid. It's a mother's job to protect her children, is it not?" she said and placed her hands on her abdomen.

"And yet you chose to stay with the man."

Abby lifted her gaze to the man. "Haven't you heard anything I've said? Pearl told me not to leave. She told me it wasn't safe. I had to find out what my husband was hiding from me." She continued without waiting for his response. "Jacob wasn't worried about the hurricane, but he knew there was a chance the power would go out, so he sent me out for supplies. While I was there, Pearl found me."

"Don't you think it odd that every time Jacob sent you to the store, Pearl just happened to show up?"

"When else was she going to find me? It wasn't like she could knock on the front door." Abby continued when Jefferies failed to comment. "Pearl was agitated this time. She was upset that Jacob knew about the baby and told me it wasn't safe for me to leave just yet."

"Why?"

"Why what?" Abby asked.

"Why wasn't it safe for Jacob to know about the baby?"

"Pearl didn't say." Okay, it wasn't a total lie. "She told me there was a storm coming, and I couldn't leave. I thought she meant the hurricane, but she told me there was another storm."

"Did you know what she meant?"

"Not at the time," Abby said, shaking her head. She had to be careful now so she didn't implicate herself or Kevin. "Pearl warned me not to evacuate. I thought it funny because, in the next breath, she told me she was leaving."

"Do as I say, not as I do," Jefferies said.

"That's pretty much what I said too, but Pearl was adamant that I stay. She told me it was the only way I would be safe. She said 'the way up is the way out.'"

"Pretty vague."

"I agree. I told her I didn't understand, but she told me it was the only way and that I'd know what it meant when the time came. She made me repeat it." Abby purposely left off the part where Pearl said only one must go up and that the baby would be born with protection, knowing it would lead to questions about why she feared for her child's safety.

"The news was telling everyone to leave. Did you ever consider not listening to her?"

"Once. Jacob saw I was concerned and asked if I wanted to go. I teetered for a moment, then recalled Pearl's words and told him no. He seemed relieved. A day and a half before the hurricane was due to hit, Jacob got a phone call that set him on his heels. I don't know what it was, but it had him worked up. He told me he needed to go take care of it and wanted to know if I wanted to go with him. He must have been worried about the storm because this was work, and Jacob never wanted to talk about that."

"You've said that before. Were you not the least bit curious about what the man did for a living? I mean, isn't it normal to want to know a little about the man you pledge to marry before tying the knot? I'm sorry, I don't mean to sound judgmental. I am just trying to understand what was going through your mind."

Sinister Winds

"You mean, how could I be so stupid?"

"Your words, not mine," Jefferies said.

"What can I say? I was screwed up. I'd lost everything. Looking back, there were plenty of red flags, but Jacob always managed to explain them away."

"What about after you were married? Did you ever ask where the money came from? Weren't you the least bit curious about what put food on the table?"

"Of course. Who wouldn't be? I asked once, and Jacob told me that curiosity killed the cat. I wasn't sure if he was talking about me or Gulliver. Either way, I knew it to be a veiled threat, so I never asked again."

"Did it ever occur to you that your husband could be a drug lord?"

"Jacob had an office in town, and he always wore nice clothes. He and Nathan talked about the dangers of acquiring the product so close to home. They realized I was listening and changed the subject."

Jefferies jotted in his book then looked in her direction. "But you've never seen anything in the house? Or saw Jacob using drugs?"

"You mean besides when he gave them to me or used them to murder my first husband?" She sighed and tempered her anger. "No, I've never seen any drugs in our home."

Jefferies jotted on the notepad once more. "Okay, so the storm's heading your way and your husband has to go attend to some mystery business. You're on your own. What happens next?"

"I went next door to get Kevin. To help me search Jacob's office," Abby said when Jefferies raised an eyebrow. She debated telling him that Merrick was parked outside and decided against it. "Jacob said he would be gone most of the day, but I was still worried he'd come home and find me snooping. I was going to call Kevin, but I wanted to see Gulliver. Anyway, Kevin is a computer whiz, and he'd been able to hack into Jacob's computer."

Jefferies thumbed through the book he'd been writing in. "When?"

"Back when I first found the key. Didn't I tell you?"

"You did not."

"Jacob left, and I called Kevin so we could look in the office. Kevin was afraid of Jacob coming home and finding the computer warm, so he downloaded everything to this little thingy he had and said he'd check it once he got home. Kevin picked the lock to the closet door and discovered a set of stairs that led to the attic. He said Jacob had to have had them custom installed because his house was identical and all he had was a pull-down staircase to the attic. The door at the top of the stairs was padlocked. He was just getting ready to pick that one too, when Jacob returned. Kevin barely made it out of the house before Jacob came in."

"How is it that your neighbor just happens to know how to pick locks?"

Abby debated telling Jefferies the truth, then decided there was no reason not to. "Kevin's dad didn't like the fact that his son was gay and used to lock him in the closet. Sometimes, his father forgot to let him out, so Kevin learned to pick the lock."

"Did Kevin find anything on the files?"

"My birth certificate and pictures of my real parents. The date was wrong and so were the names, but when he showed them to me, I knew. Jacob always told me I looked just like my mother, but I never could see it. That was because Marsha had mousy brown hair. But when Kevin showed me a picture of Clarice, it was like looking in the mirror. There wasn't anything else useful on the computer, so we started searching the room. That's when we found the hidden compartment in the bookcase. There were shoeboxes full of cash and albums with the newspaper clippings I told you about before. My purse was in there...the one that was stolen the day Eva was killed. All over a stupid purse. She'd still be alive if not for me."

"You did not kill her," Jefferies said firmly.

"Didn't I, though? Jacob said it was to teach me a lesson about following the rules. I disobey, I get punished, or someone gets killed." Abby laughed, though nothing about the situation was funny. "You want to know what Jacob's job was? He was a teacher and oh so very good at it."

"How much cash?"

Abby realized she'd started crying again and wiped at her tears with shaky hands. "A lot. At least four or five shoeboxes full. We had other things to tend to, so I didn't stop to count it."

"Like?"

"We found a set of keys and figured they fit the closet door, and we were both eager to see what else Jacob had to hide. A whole other office," she said before he could ask. "It wasn't as nice as the one downstairs but served its purpose. There was a desk, a computer with two monitors, a large sea captain's chest, and lots of file cabinets."

"Right over your head and yet you never knew it existed," Jefferies replied.

"I heard him up there once. It was the day I arrived. He claimed he was putting my suitcases away. Anyway, Kevin went to work on the computer, and I went to work trying to see if any of the keys fit the lock on the chest. They didn't, so I left Kevin to the computer and went back downstairs to search the office again."

"What did Kevin find on the computer?"

"Nothing. Jacob had it protected and Kevin didn't have time to hack the password. He got into the trunk but wouldn't let me see inside. Jacob returned before he could tell me what he'd seen." Okay, a small lie, plus she'd managed to tell the tale and leave out the part about Merrick showing up and what Kevin had done to protect her. "Kevin left that night. He tried to get me to come with him, but I had to listen to Pearl. I've talked to him twice since I've been in here, but after everything that happened, neither of us has wanted to talk about it."

"Did you confront your husband about what you'd learned?"

"Not at first. I could see something was wrong when he came home. It was his eyes," she said by way of explanation. "They always seemed to have a gold gleam when he was angry. Whenever I saw his eyes turn gold, I knew something bad was going to happen. We had dinner and went to bed. The wind from the hurricane arrived way ahead of the storm, and neither of us slept much. He was already awake when I got out of bed, and I was surprised to find the door to his office standing wide open. Jacob never left it unlocked. I questioned it, and he slapped me. It was then I knew I must have left something out of place. He was calm—too much so, and his eyes were blazing gold. In that instant, I knew what Pearl had meant about a storm coming and that it wasn't the hurricane I had to worry about."

"What did you do?"

"We'd found a pistol in the room, and Kevin insisted I keep it. I'd hid it in my drawer and went to retrieve it.

Jacob didn't think I'd use it, so I fired and hit the door jamb. That scared him. While most people waited out the hurricane, taking comfort in each other's arms, Jacob and I sat across the room from each other, each contemplating our next move. I was mentally and physically exhausted, and Jacob tried to use that to his advantage to coax me into relinquishing the gun." She yawned, just thinking about how weary she'd been. "All of a sudden, I realized my feet were wet. Jacob said the levee broke and told me we would both drown if we didn't move to higher ground." She looked at Jefferies as she said it.

"The way up is the way out," he said, repeating her earlier words.

"I made him give me his keys and went into the office and locked the door behind me. I knew he'd follow, but I hoped I could make it into the attic before he did. I couldn't get the closet door unlocked, so I shot the lock. Then, I grabbed my purse and used the keys to unlock the door to the attic. By then, Jacob had kicked in the office door."

"And you held him at gunpoint until he drowned," Jefferies answered for her.

Abby shook her head. "I didn't have the gun. I'd laid it down when I retrieved my purse. Jacob found it and started shooting through the attic floor."

"So, you did not kill your husband?" Jefferies asked.

Abby remembered Gomez's warning. "My husband drowned, Mr. Jefferies."

As Jefferies copied down her words, the hint of a smile tugged at the man's lips.

"What happens now?" Abby asked when he finally stopped writing.

"Nothing at the moment. When the water retreats, it will be easy enough to verify your story. They say dead men tell no tales, but I think this case will prove that adage is false. With any luck, the water didn't reach the attic and we'll be able to see what else your husband was hiding. If not, we'll bring your neighbor in and have him tell us what he saw."

"So, we're done?"

"Not yet."

"But you said we're good."

He nodded. "Providing your story checks out."

"It will," she assured him.

"That doesn't change the fact that the voodoo sisters still seem to think you're in danger, and for some reason, they've recruited me to help. So until you're ready to tell me what you are hiding or until I figure it out on my own, we will proceed with extreme caution. Understand?"

Abby nodded.

CHAPTER ELEVEN

Roberta entered the hospital room without knocking. "Looks like you're getting sprung," she said as she handed Abby a plastic bag.

Abby reached into the bag and pulled out a navy blue sundress with white polka dots. The dress had a built-in bra, side pockets, and thin spaghetti straps tied at the shoulder. "Pretty."

"I can't let you leave here wearing a hospital gown now, can I?" Roberta said as she removed the IV from Abby's arm and covered the area with a cotton ball and tape.

"What about the outfit I was wearing when I came in?"

Roberta wrinkled her nose. "Sure, if you want to go around smelling like ass. Obviously, you haven't bothered to open the locker over there. Seriously, you should just drop it in the trashcan and be done with it."

"At least let me pay you for the dress," Abby said.

"No need. It wasn't expensive. I picked it up at the thrift shop the other day when I was there. I washed it but didn't iron it. Hopefully, it's not too wrinkled."

Abby ran a hand along the dress. "It's fine. Thank you."

Roberta nodded to the bag. "There's a pair of

underwear in the bag. Don't worry; those are new, but I did wash them. And no, you don't owe me anything."

"Thank you."

"Hey, no problem. You just promise to take care of yourself and that baby of yours."

"That's the plan," Abby said. "So, what, I just leave?"

"Yep. I'll call for the orderly to wheel you down."

Abby raised an eyebrow. "Wheel me down?"

Roberta shrugged. "Hospital policy."

"What about the paperwork?"

"Already taken care of."

"What do you mean taken care of? By who?"

"I don't know. When I went to print off your discharge papers, it said complete. It was probably a computer glitch. Count your blessings. You've been in a private room for over a week, and that bill would be a doozy. Now get yourself dressed, and I'll call for the orderly."

Abby's fear that Jacob somehow managed to get out of the house and survive the flood played to her anxiety of hearing her hospital bill was taken care of. Her hands trembled as she changed out of the hospital gown and worked to adjust the straps on the sundress. Roberta had a good eye. The dress was a nearly perfect fit. It was a bit loose, but nothing another week or two of being pregnant wouldn't fix.

Abby moved to the sink, looked in the mirror, and forced herself to watch as she pulled the plastic comb provided by the hospital through her brilliant red hair. She never minded looking in the mirror before, but now each time she did, she was reminded of what Jacob had done to her birth mother. The knowledge did nothing to ease her anxiety.

She slipped into the sandals and went to the locker to

retrieve her purse. She lifted the plastic bag from the hook, looked inside, and gagged as the smell reached her nostrils, flooding her with memories of her time in the attic, clawing her way to safety and then waiting on the hot tar roof for help to arrive. Every little noise caused her to draw into herself as the guilt of what she had done mingled with the fear of not having accomplished the task. Even now, as she stood there staring into the bag, she didn't know the answer. Until she did, there would always be the fear of her past catching up with her, especially when she recalled his last words.

Regardless of whether his bitter words were an attempt to continue to control her from the grave or to warn her of impending danger, he'd succeeded in enforcing the fear that had surrounded her since she'd become his wife. She clenched her jaw as she forcefully slammed the bag of clothes in the trashcan. Steadying herself, she pulled her purse from the top shelf and felt a new wave of grief as she felt the weight of the bag and was once more reminded of the dangerous secret she kept. "Damn you, Jacob Buckley! I hope you rot in hell!" A chill raced along her spine as she heard a noise behind her and knew she was no longer alone in the room. She turned and saw Jefferies standing just inside the door to her room, his fingers wrapped around the handles of the wheelchair he'd rolled in without her hearing.

Though she knew he was privy to her recent outburst, he merely smiled and motioned toward the chair. "Ready to go?"

She breathed a sigh. Something about the man's presence seemed to calm the jitters that a second before threatened to cripple her. She forced a smile. "If you're going to moonlight as an orderly, you might want to rethink your wardrobe. Some might find the three-piece suit a bit intimidating."

"I heard you were going to be released and thought you might need a lift," Jefferies said, motioning toward the chair. "I used to push my grandfather around on occasion. I'm a bit rusty, but I promise to do my best not to run you into any walls."

Abby took a chance. "You wouldn't know anything about my hospital account being taken care of, would you?"

"Sometimes things just have a way of working themselves out," he replied.

"I'll take that as a yes," she said, settling into the chair. "Where are you taking me?"

"Where were you planning on going if I hadn't shown up?" Jefferies asked, wheeling her from the room.

"I was thinking about going to Virginia to get my cat if I'm allowed to leave the state."

"Everything we've discussed has been completely off the record at this point. And from what you've said, I see no reason to hold you . What are your plans after that?"

"I don't guess I've given it much thought. Kevin said I can stay in their guest room if I want. It wouldn't be permanent, but maybe just until I can sleep without being afraid of waking up and finding Jacob hovering over my bed."

"Their house?"

"He's staying at his dad's house."

"This is the guy who used to lock him in the closet?"

"Kevin said he's changed," Abby said over her shoulder.

"If you get there and find yourself fearing for your safety, you give me a call," Jefferies said, stopping at the elevator. "Also, to your point, I aim to stay in the area until I can get in the house and put eyes on the man's body. I'm not sure it will fully alleviate your worries, but you would be able to take the possibility of his imminent return out of the equation."

"Thank you." The elevator doors opened, and Jefferies wheeled her inside. "The television said it could take months or years to get things back to normal. Do you know how long it will be before they allow you into the area?"

"Our agency lives by a different set of rules. It shouldn't be much longer," he promised once the doors closed.

Even though the elevator ride down was quick, Abby felt her shoulders relax the moment the doors opened. Jefferies wheeled her into the hallway, stopping halfway down the hall and handing her an envelope. Abby looked inside to find a plane ticket with her name on it to Norfolk, Virginia. "How? I only told you a few moments ago."

"I didn't see as you had many options. I've called you a cab. It should be waiting out front. The driver will see that you get to the airport safely."

"You're not taking me?"

"No. We both know you don't fully trust me. A cab is better for both you and the baby. You need to relax and take care of the little one. Stress isn't good for the baby."

"Mr. Jefferies?"

"Yes?"

"I really want to trust you."

"I know." His hand came to rest on her shoulder, and she felt her shoulder tense under the warmth of it. He must have felt her tension, as he quickly removed it. He pulled out his wallet and offered her five twenties.

Abby shook her head. "No, you've done enough. I

don't need your money."

"Use it to pay the cab driver and for any purchases in the airport." He pressed the money into her hand, eyed the purse sitting in her lap, and handed her another card with his name and number on it. "Wait until the cab is moving, then keep the bag low and remove your ID. Place it in your pocket with the money I just gave you, and don't open that bag unless you have to. If anyone sees what's inside, you'll make yourself a target."

She swallowed. Obviously, Jefferies knew she'd filled her purse with money during her escape. "You know?" she said and clutched her purse tighter.

"I didn't until just now."

"I know it's dirty money. I didn't take it all. I just thought it would help me take care of my baby," Abby said softly.

"You didn't do anything anyone in the same circumstances wouldn't have done," Jefferies assured her. "I doubt there's any record of how much cash was there. And with all the reports of looting, who's to say there will even be any left in the house when we get there."

She felt tears well in her eyes. When she spoke, her words came out in a whisper. "Thank you."

"Yes, ma'am." He stood and stepped behind the chair. "Now, let's get you going before you miss your flight."

***

Abby felt a pang of anxiety as she placed her purse, shoes, and phone into the plastic bin and watched it roll up the conveyor belt. The man sitting behind the conveyor's eyes bugged as he peered into the monitor. He called another man over and pointed to the screen. The man looked up and saw her watching, then followed the bag to the end.

Sinister Winds

She half expected him to stop her from retrieving it. When he didn't, she looped the strap around her neck and leaned closer so that she could be heard. "I was in the hurricane. I wasn't sure what to expect, so I emptied my bank account just in case. It's a good thing I did because it destroyed my house," Abby said, repeating the advice Jefferies had given her just before opening the door to the cab.

A frown tugged at the man's face. "Smart thinking. I bet others are wishing they'd done the same thing," he said, lifting the empty tray out of the way.

"Indeed," Abby said and turned without another word. Pulling the bag in front of her, she checked her ticket once more and then proceeded to her gate as the overhead speaker announced boarding for first class. Abby checked her ticket, surprised to see herself included in the early boarding. She got in line and handed the woman at the counter her ticket and waited for her to hand it back. She found her seat and had only been seated for a moment when a woman in a dark suit stopped beside her chair. Her hair was pulled up into a tight bun, and she pressed a small suitcase into the overhead compartment and then took the empty aisle seat beside Abby.

The woman started to release the tray from the back of the seat in front of her and glanced over at Abby. "Do you want me to put your bag in the overhead?"

Abby shook her head. "No, I'll keep my purse with me."

"First time flying?"

Abby nodded.

"You'll have to put it under the seat. They won't let you keep it in your lap when the plane takes off," she said, releasing the tray.

Abby placed the bag on the floor and used her feet to slide it under the seat.

"I'll have a screwdriver," the woman said when the flight attendant approached. The woman sitting beside her looked over at Abby. "What's your guilty pleasure? Drinks come with your first-class ticket," she said when Abby hesitated.

"No alcohol," Abby replied.

A knowing look passed over the woman's face as she glanced at Abby's stomach. "They have ginger ale."

"That works," Abby said, bobbing her head.

"And cookies," the woman said as the attendant was turning to leave. She glanced at Abby once more. "You do like cookies, right?"

"Yes."

"Sorry, I didn't mean to come across so strong. I'm a frequent flyer for my business and was just trying to help."

Abby started to ask what the woman did for a living but didn't want to appear nosey. Besides, the truth of the matter was she didn't really care. She just wanted to get to Virginia and see a friendly face. She pulled the phone from her pocket to text Kevin. > *"Sorry to spring this on you at the last minute, but I'm on my way to see you. If the offer to stay at your place still stands, I'll take you up on it; if not, please recommend a good hotel."* She hit send and waited for a reply.

Kevin >"You are not staying in a hotel, and that is final! What time does your flight get in?"

Abby sent another text giving him the info and looked to see her seat mate watching. She felt her face flush.

The woman laughed. "Honey, either you're young and in love, or I just caught you sneaking a text to your secret lover."

"I'm pregnant. I assure you there are no secret lovers in my future," Abby said dryly.

The woman frowned. "Seriously? When I was pregnant, all I wanted was sex. You're saying you haven't experienced the pregnancy hormones yet?"

Abby shook her head. "I can't say that I have."

"Oh, you will, and when you do, they are divine."

"My husband is dead." Abby regretted the statement the moment she said it.

"Oh, honey. I'm so sorry. What happened?"

"He drowned in the hurricane."

"Katrina?"

"Yes."

"Oh, you poor thing. That is just awful. Was your house destroyed?"

Abby shrugged. "I guess. It was underwater."

"So, what, you evacuated?"

"No, my husband didn't want to." Abby wasn't sure why she felt the need to answer. Perhaps it was just because it had been too long since she'd spoken to another woman besides Pearl, but since she rarely got a word in, she didn't think that counted. She watched as the rest of the passengers filed onboard and grew quiet when the attendant returned with their drinks and several packages of wafer cookies.

"Where are you headed?" the woman asked as soon as the attendant left.

"Virginia," Abby said, leaving out the exact location. "I have a little layover in Atlanta."

"Have you ever been to the Atlanta airport? Of course, you haven't; you said this is your first time flying. You'll barely have time to go to the bathroom before boarding the next flight. You know, I think it must be fate we are sitting right next to each other. Don't you worry about a thing. I've been to Atlanta a zillion times and know my way around. I'll get us to the gate on time." The woman grew quiet as the flight attendant came on the speaker, gave a welcome speech, and explained the emergency procedures. "Don't let it scare you. I've flown a zillion times and haven't crashed yet."

Abby laughed. "That's what my husband said about the hurricane. Don't worry, Abigail, I've been through plenty of hurricanes; there's nothing to them. Famous last words."

"Yeah, well, don't you worry, Abigail. It's not my time to go nor yours either."

"Abby."

"What?"

"Only my husband called me Abigail."

"Oh, I'm sorry. My name's Belinda Winters. Does it hurt much?"

"What, hearing my name?" Abby asked.

"No, being without him."

"I guess I'm still in shock. I didn't get to see his body, so a part of me wonders if he's still alive." Okay, that was a pretty good answer.

"You said he drowned. How do you know?"

"The levee broke, and the water started coming in. I was scared and went into the attic," Abby said, reliving the time. "I waited in there for a while. It was so hot, I could barely breathe; my husband never came up. I don't know how long I stayed there wondering what he was up to, and then I noticed my feet were getting wet. It scared me. I looked out the window, and there was water everywhere. I didn't want to drown, and I was worried about the baby, so I climbed out the window and onto the roof." *Oh for the love of God. Why don't you just go ahead and tell the woman you killed the man,* Abby said to herself, berating herself for being so chatty.

"That was incredibly brave."

"I didn't have any other choice," Abby said truthfully. The plane picked up speed, and Abby held on to the arms of her seat as it lifted into the air.

"There, that wasn't so bad, was it?" Belinda said.

"No."

"It's a short flight. We'll be on the ground before you know it. Now, tell me about this guy you're going to meet. He is a guy, right? What is he, your old boyfriend?"

Abby laughed. "Yes, he's a guy. No, he's not an old boyfriend."

"Oh, how intriguing. A new boyfriend, then? Sorry, I guess I'm a hopeless romantic. I read a lot and am a sucker for happy endings."

Abby found herself wishing the woman had chosen to read on the flight instead of wanting a replay of her life story. "No happy endings for me. Kevin is gay."

"A little gay or a lot gay?"

Abby laughed despite herself. "Is there a difference?"

The woman lowered her voice. "Sure, there is. I have a friend who says he's gay, but that doesn't stop him from experimenting. I find gay men to be excellent kissers. Maybe it's because they're so in touch with their feminine side. So, come on, surely the two of you have had some kind of thing going."

Abby started to tell her the man helped her get out of an abusive relationship, but Pearl's words floated to the surface. *No trust stranger.* She'd thought that meant men, but here she was, spilling her guts to someone she'd just met. "Kevin is a friend and nothing more. To be honest, he's the only one I have in the world. He offered to take my cat with him when he evacuated. I agreed. I am going to get my cat. I'm sorry to disappoint you, but I assure you that's all there is to it."

"Do you think you'll return to New Orleans?"

"No. There's nothing left for me there. I'm sorry, but it's been a long day. I'm going to close my eyes for a while."

"Sure thing, honey. You go right ahead."

Abby opened her eyes as the fasten seatbelt sign blinked off.

"You must have been tired. You missed the landing. I was going to wake you, but you were sleeping so soundly," Belinda said, unfastening her belt. She stood blocking the aisle as she pulled her bag from the overhead compartment. She placed the bag in the seat with a huff and looked over at Abby. "Which one is yours? I'll grab it for you."

"I don't have a carry-on."

"No?"

"Nope, just my purse." Abby bent and pulled it from under the seat.

Belinda eyed the bag. "No wonder. That thing is so packed full, it looks like it's going to split open. Here, hand it to me, and I'll wrap it around my carry-on. It's got wheels, and that bag looks heavy."

"Um, that's okay. I can carry my own bag," Abby told her.

"Are you sure? We're going to the same gate. I really don't mind."

"I can carry my own bag," Abby repeated.

Belinda pulled her bag from the seat, lowered it to the aisle, elbowed her way back a couple of steps, and motioned Abby into the aisle. For a moment, Abby considered resisting but decided the woman hadn't actually done anything but offer to help. Besides, her purse was indeed as heavy as it looked and, as such, would make an excellent weapon if warranted.

CHAPTER TWELVE

After the short flight from Alanta to Norfolk, Abby stared out the window, watching as the plane landed, did a slight hop, and touched down once more. As it continued along the runway, the chimes of multiple cell phones rang through the cabin followed by the hum of voices speaking into their phones. Abby powered up her phone and texted Kevin to let him know her plane had landed, then stuffed the phone in her pocket and pulled her purse from under the seat, clutching it tight in front of her as the plane rolled to a stop. Abby watched as passengers rose and began pulling bags from the overhead compartments. Not too long ago, she'd arrived in New Orleans thinking she'd hit bottom with everything she had to her name stuffed into the confines of her car. Now, everything she owned was stuffed into the bag sitting in her lap. Granted, there was enough cash in the bag to buy anything she needed, but she couldn't stop thinking that the cash was tainted. A part of her had actually been disappointed when Jefferies didn't try to confiscate it. *Cheer up, Abby, you're scraping the bottom of the barrel; there's nowhere to go but up from here.*

The man who'd been sitting next to her stood, saw her

looking, and motioned her out in front of him.

"Thank you," Abby said, sliding out of her seat and following the line to exit the plane.

Belinda was waiting for her when she reached the waiting area and stepped up beside her as she walked. "The luggage area is this way. Take your time, it'll be a few moments before the bags reach the turnstile."

"I don't have any bags," Abby reminded her.

Belinda's eyes grew round. "Shit, girl, I thought you just meant no carry-on."

"Nope." Abby laughed and waved a hand across her body. "This is everything I own."

"You've lost your husband, had to be rescued by helicopter, and have nothing but the clothes on your back. I'm telling you, girl, I would be much more upset than you seem to be," Belinda replied.

"I've cried a million tears in the last week. It doesn't do anything but give me bags under my eyes." Something Belinda said nagged at her. She stopped walking and turned to the woman. "How did you know about the helicopter?"

"ABBY!"

Abby looked to see a flash of pink at the end of the restricted – passengers only hallway. Tears sprang to her eyes at the sight of Kevin wielding a sign that read *Welcome Home, Sunshine*. They embraced, remaining intertwined for several moments as the stress of everything she'd been through melted away. Finally, she pulled back and was glad to see she wasn't the only one blubbering like a baby. She looked for Belinda, thinking to introduce them, but the woman was nowhere to be seen. She turned her attention back to Kevin. "I've never been so happy to see anyone in my whole life."

"Me too, Sunshine. You look a bit pale, though. I think I may have to find a new name for you," he said, eyeing her critically.

"It's just from being in the hospital for over a week. You can't get much of a tan from a hospital bed," she said as they began walking.

Kevin gave her a worried glance. "Are you sure everything is okay with the baby?"

"Relax, Kevin, everything is fine. It was just dehydration. They gave me fluids and the baby's heart rate is fine now. That's why they kept me so long, to make sure we were both okay."

He let out a sigh. "As long as you're sure."

"They would not have let me fly if they didn't think I would be okay," she said to reassure him.

"This way to the baggage claim," he said with a tilt of the head.

"No baggage," she said, patting her purse.

He eyed the bag dubiously. "Well, I wasn't going to say anything, but the bag is hideous. I hope you have a change of underwear at least."

"Nope. Just a hospital toothbrush, a few hair essentials, and a cheap comb. I don't even have a change of clothes." She felt her lips quiver.

Kevin, seeing her distress, took her by the arm. "Don't you worry, Sunshine; we have some great malls around here. We'll get your closet full in no time." Kevin's face became serious. "You're what matters, not things. Things can be replaced."

"I know."

"Then you should also know that I'm glad you and the baby are safe. I will take care of you now," he said, pulling her arm through his and escorting her from the building.

As they walked, Abby had the feeling of being watched.

***

Abby was exhausted by the time they finally made it to the house. They'd stopped by Lynnhaven Mall so she could pick up enough clothes to keep her going for a few weeks and two new pink shirts for Kevin before heading to the Great Bridge section of Chesapeake. As Kevin drove through the older neighborhood with large, established trees, it crossed Abby's mind that it looked like a perfect neighborhood. She was quick to remind herself that nothing was ever perfect. She would never fall under that assumption again. Nothing was as it seemed and there were no Norman Rockwell neighborhoods in real life.

"This is it," Kevin said, pulling into the driveway of a single-story red brick ranch with black shutters. "Doesn't look as if Dad is home."

"Good, it will give me time to take a shower," she said, relieved. She wasn't looking forward to meeting the man who'd locked Kevin in the closet as a boy, even if she was grateful for the skills he'd gleaned from the experience.

"Relax, Sunshine. Dad is an okay guy."

Abby rolled her eyes. "So I've heard."

"He's mellowed with age," Kevin said, opening the trunk and pulling out several clothing bags.

She followed him into the house and stood in stunned silence, staring at the décor. Green carpet, bold curtains with oversized flowers, and a black and white plaid couch.

Kevin shrugged his shoulders at her unspoken comment. "I've begged him to let me remodel, but he refuses. I think he's afraid I'll make it too gay."

"Like anything can be worse than this," Abby said with a flourish of the hand.

121

"His taste is all in his mouth," Kevin said, flipping on the turquoise lamp.

"It's like a garage sale vomited in here," Abby agreed.

The couch cushion moved. Abby peered closer. "Gulliver?"

The cat rolled onto his back and meowed a soulful cry.

"What on earth is the matter with him?" she asked, her voice etched with fear.

"Too many donuts," Kevin said with a sigh.

"Shit, Kevin!" Abby said, staring at the lethargic feline.

"Not me, Dad. He found out Gulliver likes donuts and thinks it's fun to watch him eat them." He sat the bags down. "In the old man's defense, he's never had a cat before."

The second Abby reached him, Gulliver let out a barrage of feline cries, head-butting against her and purring his contentment. A sea of tears rolled down her face, falling onto the oblivious cat. "Oh, Gulliver," she sobbed. "I didn't think I would ever see you again."

Kevin joined her on the couch. "I guess maybe he's been depressed and drowning his sorrows in jelly donuts I've not seen him this excited in weeks," he said with a twinge of guilt.

Abby tried to hold back the tears, but the effort was futile. Once opened, the floodgates refused to close. It was the first time since her wedding that she truly felt safe. She was still sobbing long after Gulliver had settled peacefully in her lap.

Kevin left the room and came back holding two bottles of water and a box of Kleenex. He handed her one of the water bottles and the box of tissues, which she gratefully accepted.

He sat beside her, opened his water, and took a drink.

Sinister Winds

She leaned against him in companionable silence until her tears subsided.

"Something tells me this is not just about jelly donuts," he said at last.

They had only spoken twice during the time she was in the hospital. Kevin did not know of the events that took place after his departure. He had not asked, and she had not offered. Abby struggled to find her voice, afraid the words would bring a new onslaught of tears.

"Jacob is dead," she said, her voice trembling.

"I know. If he was alive, he would have found you by now," he said, taking a swig of his water.

"I killed him, Kevin."

He nodded. "The gun?"

"No, I tried, but in the end, I couldn't pull the trigger."

"Probably for the best; a gunshot wound is pretty hard to explain, even if it is self-defense," he said practically. "If you didn't shoot him, then how?"

"Remember when Pearl said the way up is the way out? Well, when the water came in, I knew what she meant. I went upstairs and pulled the trunk over the opening so he couldn't get up. The water was in the house by then, and he drowned," she said, explaining the events of the day.

"Wait, you moved that trunk? By yourself? That thing had to weigh at least a hundred pounds," he said incredulously. "How in the heck did you move it?"

"I've been asking myself that for weeks. I keep reliving it over and over. I told Mr. Jefferies the truth, but every time I see a cop, I'm afraid they've come to arrest me. He said everything I told him was off the record, but what if he was lying?" she said, sobbing out a fresh wave of tears. "I mean, I didn't shoot him, but my fingerprints are on the gun. What if they decide the bullet holes are enough to arrest me for attempted murder?"

"Bullet holes? I thought you said you didn't shoot him?"

"I didn't. I shot the closet door," she said, blowing her nose.

"Why would you shoot the closet door?"

She nudged him with her shoulder. "Because you weren't there to pick the lock."

Kevin laughed. "Silly me for leaving during a hurricane. I guess we should have worked on your sleuthing skills." He was quiet for a moment. "Okay, so the cops come in, find the body, and then find the trunk over the opening. Maybe the water got so high the trunk floated over the opening?"

"No, I wasn't sure at first, but from what I've seen on the news, it's not likely the water got much higher than the floorboards of the attic. Besides, I moved the trunk back before I left."

"You moved it twice? How?"

She shrugged. "I have no clue. I honestly don't remember the first time, but the second time took some doing."

"Remind me not to mess with you," Kevin replied.

"I'm scared, Kevin. I know what Mr. Jefferies said, but I don't want to have this baby in jail."

Kevin took hold of her hand. "There is no way they can prove you blocked his exit. Look at you. You're pregnant. Even if you weren't, the trunk weighs nearly as much as you. Your husband drowned. So, technically, you did not kill him."

"I helped..."

"You did not kill your husband. He died like many other unfortunate souls during that awful storm," he said, cutting her off.

"But…"

"Your husband drowned, Abby," he said more firmly.

She nodded.

"Now say it."

"My husband drowned," she said.

He squeezed her hand. "That's right. Now you put that guilt to bed, Sunshine. You know as well as I do that he would have pulled the trigger if the roles were reversed."

She hadn't thought about it like that. Kevin was right. Even knowing she was in the attic, Jacob didn't hesitate to shoot through the floorboards. If he had killed her, he would have told himself it was her fault for making him do it—saying she should have played by the rules. She let out a sigh. Her whole life had been one big game of chess, with Jacob moving the pieces. "You sound like Gomez," she said. She told him about her rescue and the conversation with the man while in the chopper. "You would have liked him."

Kevin sighed. "Sounds like a dream date."

She laughed. "Spin it all you like, Kev. It was more like a nightmare."

Kevin placed an arm around her shoulders. "You're going to be okay. You're safe now. You and your bundle of joy. Jacob's dead, you have a friend in the FBI, and no one's going to ever hurt you or your baby again."

She must have gone white because Kevin jumped off the couch and hovered over her like a mother hen.

"What is it?" he said, his voice rising.

"The baby!"

Kevin's eyes darted to her stomach as his voice rose a whole octave. "What, are you in labor again? Oh God, it's too early for that. Isn't it?"

Gulliver jumped up with a hiss.

"Kevin, sit down. You're scaring Gulliver. I'm not in labor," she said firmly.

"Then what is it?" he insisted as he sat next to her once more. "You look like you are going to pass out."

"It's the baby. Jacob has already sold it. He took a deposit for it. I told him to call the person, but the phone lines were dead. What if they find me? What if they try to take my baby?" She could feel her anxiety building, but she couldn't control it. She reached for the purse and opened it for him to see.

Kevin looked inside the purse and cocked his head. "You're walking around with that and you let me pay for your clothes?"

"I couldn't chance opening the purse at the mall. Besides, I told you I'll pay you back."

"I'm not worried about that. I was just giving you a hard time. You didn't tell your FBI friend about the cash?"

"He knows I took some, but not how much. He knows it was ill-gotten, but not how. Maybe I should have told him about Jacob selling our baby."

"Perhaps, but then again, I've always felt it best to follow your gut, and for some reason, your momma bear instincts told you not to." Kevin placed his hands on her shoulders and held her gaze. "Abby, you are my best friend, and that baby is probably the closest I will ever come to having a child of my own. I will protect it like a mother tigress protects her cubs."

"No, I can't stay here. It's too dangerous. This is my mess, not yours. I can't ask you to get involved," Abby protested.

Kevin firmed his grip on her shoulders, his eyes pleading with hers. "I got involved the minute I smashed the lamp over the goon's head. In case you've forgotten, I killed a man for you. I can only hope the flood washed him away, but if not... Bottom line, we are in this together. You, me, and our baby!"

"Ahem."

Kevin let go of her shoulders and scrambled to his feet to face the man who'd just entered. Aside from the plucked eyebrows, spiked hair, and a preference for pink clothing, there was a slight resemblance between the two.

Kevin smiled at Abby. "Abby, this is my dad, Edward Bishop. Dad, this is Abby. She is going to be staying here for a bit."

This was obviously news to the man, who arched an unmanicured brow and spoke in a decidedly lower voice. "Is that so?"

"Yes, just until we find a place to stay," Kevin assured him. "We'll be taking Gulliver with us."

"We'll discuss all of that later. First, I'd like to know a bit about the mother of my grandchild." Edward glanced at Abby's stomach and then directed his attention to his son. "Since it looks as though we still have a bit of time to deal with that, I reckon we'll start by having you tell me about the dead body you left in New Orleans and why I am just now hearing about it."

"That would be bodies," Abby corrected.

To his credit, the man did not flinch. Of course not. Kevin said he was a retired police officer; the man had probably heard it all. Abby watched as he pulled up a chair, turned it around, and sat facing them.

"Let's take this from the beginning," Edward said in a steady voice that spoke of years of practice.

CHAPTER THIRTEEN

Abby spent the better part of an hour telling Edward and Kevin everything she could recall from the moment she'd arrived in New Orleans until her arrival in Virginia. While she'd left out some key points when telling the story to Jefferies, as painful as the truth was, she didn't hold back this time. Both Kevin and Edward remained silent, only weighing in when they needed something she said clarified. "God, how could I have been so stupid?" she said when she'd finished. "Looking back, there were so many red flags."

"Don't beat yourself up, Little Missy. The man was a master manipulator. You saw only what he wanted you to see," Edward said.

"You should have asked me. I could have told you the man was a Dick," Kevin said sourly.

Edward shot his son a dirty look and then turned his attention to Abby once more. "I've heard a lot of strange things on the job, but this one takes the cake. I can see where your man Jefferies would be unsettled. We are taught to think outside the box, but I don't remember this scenario being taught at the academy. I've heard of guys dreaming about their cases or having victims haunt their

Sinister Winds

dreams, but this ... this is beyond anything I've ever experienced."

"That's because it's voodoo, Dad. You wouldn't know, because you've never been to New Orleans. God knows I've tried to get you to come for a visit."

"That's enough, Kevin," Edward replied.

Kevin crossed his legs and wrapped his slender fingers around his knees. "I'm just saying that maybe if you'd have come, you might have a better feel for the black magic."

Edward started to comment. Abby cut him off. "Kevin, why don't you tell your father what happened to Merrick?" It wasn't that she needed or wanted to hear the details of the man's demise, but something told her Edward needed to know how far his son had gone to protect her.

Kevin uncrossed his legs and leaned forward in his chair. As he spoke, his hands moved to emphasize each sordid detail. "I knew something was wrong just by the sound of Abby's voice, so I tiptoed to the front window. Sure enough, the goon was no longer in his car. I knew he must be inside, and that if I came down, he'd kill us both. Obviously, I didn't want that to happen, so I went out the window. I shim…I mean, jumped to the porch and used the front pillars to climb down. My foot hit one of the planters and I knew I was done for. I held my breath, but the goon never came out. I snuck inside and heard him saying God-awful things to poor Abby, and that's when I bashed him over the head with the lamp." Kevin grew tall in his chair, wiggling with delight. "I'm not going to lie, that felt good! I mean, that guy put off some seriously scary vibes."

Abby nodded her agreement. "Then what happened?"

"We couldn't very well leave him there, so I dragged him into my backyard." Kevin looked at his dad and wagged his finger. "Don't give me that look. The creep weighed a ton. At least I didn't leave him in Abby's backyard. I was just going to leave him there, but I've seen too many horror movies where the dead guy gets back up and kills everyone. I figured I'd get back there and find Abby dead because the guy woke up and came back to finish the job."

"What'd you do?" Edward asked when Kevin grew quiet.

"I killed him," Kevin said softly. "I clubbed him with a tree branch, then positioned it to look like it fell on the guy as he was escaping."

Edward's brow furrowed. "Escaping from what?"

"I put on his ballcap and moved his car to a driveway the next street over. I knocked but didn't get an answer. I went to the back of the house, broke a window, then rummaged around a bit. When I left, I cut through to my backyard in case anyone was watching. That's where the body is, so I figured it would add up if they were."

Edward nodded his approval. "There's no way that body's still going to be there. It's either been eaten by wildlife or drifted off to some other location. You did good, son."

"You mean except for killing a man?" Kevin's voice had lost all hint of jubilation.

"You did what you had to do. It might have been better if you'd left the man lie where you first subdued him and called the cops so they could arrest him."

Abby shook her head. "No, Jacob has friends in high places. They would have gotten him out and had Merrick kill both of us or, worse, make him kill Kevin while I watched. I'm telling you, Mr. Bishop, my husband took great pleasure in seeing me suffer."

Edward rolled his neck. "It's probably a good thing the man is dead, or I'd probably have to kill him myself."

Abby blew out a long breath. "I'm so sorry. Not only was I stupid enough to fall for Jacob's lies, but now I've gotten both of you involved."

"It's okay, Abby," Kevin told her.

She shook her head. "No, it's not. I should have told Mr. Jefferies everything. I'm going to call a cab and go to a hotel. I'll fill him in on everything I left out as soon as I'm settled."

"I'm going with you," Kevin proclaimed.

"Neither of you are going anywhere. There is safety in numbers, and I intend to see to it that my grandchild remains safe!" Edward said heatedly.

"Your grandchild?" both Abby and Kevin exclaimed at once.

"Hey, if Kevin gets to be the dad, then that makes me the grandpa," Edward said, leaving little room for objection. "Oh, and Abby, you can call me Dad; it will be less confusing for the kid."

Abby started to protest. While the man seemed amicable at the moment, there was still the fact that he'd locked his own son in the closet many times just because the boy was different. Then again, Kevin's dad hadn't sold him to the highest bidder, nor had he raised him to spend his life with a monster. Instead of agreeing outright, she smiled and nodded.

"Good, it's settled. I'll make some unofficial inquiries into the situation. I'm not sure how much I'll be able to find out about an out-of-state case, if there even is one."

Abby looked at Kevin and then back at his father. "You don't think so?"

"No. Not yet anyway. Not if this Jefferies guy let you

go. My gut tells me the man was freaked out about the whole dream visit and wanted to try to make sense of it. But if he's any sort of human being, he's going to see this for what it was."

"Which is?" Kevin asked.

"That the guy was an evil prick that the world is better off without. They both were," he said, looking at Kevin. "Don't you dare lose any sleep over what you did. I can assure you that almost everyone I know would have done the same thing. Or not. To be honest, I'm not sure everyone would have picked up on the fact that the guy was in the house. Had you gone to see what Abby wanted, I would be left thinking that you died in the hurricane."

Abby yawned.

Edward nodded to the other room. "You've had a long day, Little Missy. You go on to bed. I want to talk to my son in private if you don't mind."

Abby stood and looked at them each in turn. "Thank you both for everything." She started toward her room; Gulliver followed, weaving in and out between her feet as she walked down the hall.

***

Abby woke after a fretful night of tossing, turning, and jumping at every little noise. When she'd finally given in to sleep, it was watery dreams that kept her company. In the end, she woke feeling even more tired than when she'd gone to bed.

"Oh, Sunshine, we need to do something about those dark circles," Kevin said when she entered the kitchen.

Abby groaned in response as her gaze swept the counter in search of the coffee pot. She reached for it, then sniffed the pot before topping off Kevin's half-full mug. She returned the pot to the coffeemaker and poured herself

Sinister Winds

some orange juice. Gulliver reached his paws to her upper leg, letting out a questioning meow. She looked over at his bowl of uneaten food. "Your food is in the bowl, young man."

Gulliver sank to the floor, meowing his displeasure. Reconsidering his options, he jumped onto Kevin's lap.

"I guess it's safe to assume you're not a morning person," Kevin said, stroking the feline.

"I just need to sleep," she grumbled, watching as Kevin fed part of his breakfast sandwich to the cat. She took a drink of her juice. "I thought we were not going to feed him table food."

"Oh?" Kevin said, raising his eyebrows. "I thought you only said no donuts."

She sighed as she took a seat at the table. "Kevin, he has gained more weight than I have."

Kevin raised an eyebrow.

"I've killed once. Don't make me do it again," she warned.

"I wouldn't dream of it," he assured her. "I take it you didn't sleep well?"

She shook her head and lifted her glass, wishing it was filled with something that included caffeine.

"Care to talk about it?" he asked.

Her free hand traveled by instinct to her stomach as she felt the baby kick. "Just dreams."

A horn honked. Abby sat her glass on the table and hurried to the living room. A car was idling along the curb across the street. The horn sounded once more. Seconds later, a teenage girl bounded out of the house next door, crossed the street, and got into the waiting car. Relaxing, she turned from the window. Kevin was standing in the doorway holding Gulliver. Their eyes met.

"They're gone, Abby, both of them. They can't hurt you," he assured her.

Abby forced a smile and rubbed her arms. "I know. I just have a feeling that it's not over yet. He sold our baby, Kevin. The person who bought her is still out there, and I don't have a clue who it is. They could walk right up to me, and I'd never know it until it was too late."

Kevin walked to the couch, lowered the cat onto the cushion, and turned, placing his hands on her shoulders. "Yes, but you're not alone now. You have me and Dad now. Neither of us will let anyone hurt you or your baby."

Abby placed her hand against Kevin's cheek. "I know you both want to help, but you can't be by my side every minute."

He took her hand, kissing the palm. "You're right. Dad told me to get you a dog. He said it would help you relax and alert you if anyone comes near."

She glanced at Gulliver. "I'm not sure how he'd feel about that."

"He'll be fine as long as we get one that's good with cats," Kevin said, being practical.

She was still a bit apprehensive. "But what if the dog chases Gulliver?"

"Aren't you the one who said the cat needs to lose weight? A little exercise won't hurt him."

***

Edward scrutinized the dog Abby and Kevin, mostly Kevin, had just adopted from the shelter. After several moments, he closed his eyes, waited, and then opened them once more, looking at the dog as if surprised to see it still there. "I think you missed the point of getting a dog," he said, shaking his head.

Abby smiled as Kevin clutched the small, fluffy white

Sinister Winds

dog to his chest. "And just what is wrong with Tiffy?" he asked with an edge to his voice.

Edward placed two fingers on the bridge of his nose. "Don't start, Kevin. There is nothing wrong with the dog. It is just that the whole point of getting a dog was for protection, not to see how many times Tiffy could piddle on the carpet."

Kevin squared his shoulders. "The lady at the SPCA assured me Tiffy would be a good guard dog." As if to prove his point, Tiffy yipped a high-pitched bark. The yip was followed by a hiss from Gulliver, who had jumped onto the couch for a better view of the shaggy mut. The dog jumped from Kevin's arms, landing on the couch just short of where Gulliver stood. Gulliver arched his back, swatting at the pooch. Tiffy snapped at Gulliver, who took off running down the hall with Tiffy snarling closely behind.

"At least the dog will let you know when the cat is in the room," Edward said dryly.

Kevin glared at his dad then followed after the duo without further comment.

"You seem to really like my son," Edward said, turning his attention to Abby. It was the first opportunity they'd had to speak alone.

"Kevin is a really good friend," Abby said.

Edward sighed his disappointment. "I was hoping there was more to it than that."

"Kevin is a good guy."

"I know. I just don't know where I went wrong with the boy," he said, lowering himself into the gold recliner.

Abby stared unbelievingly. "Wrong?"

"You know, to make him turn out the way he did," he said, glancing down the hall.

Abby was incredulous. "You mean gay?"

The man nodded.

"Well, locking him in the closet may not have been the best solution." The words were out before she could stop them. Kevin's recounting of the ordeal had infuriated her at the time, and now confronted with the man who had treated her friend with such contempt, she lashed out.

"Told you about that, did he? I guess I just had trouble dealing with things back in the day," Edward replied.

"Think about how he felt," Abby hissed.

A frown fleeted across Edward's face. "I do. I have done a great deal of soul-searching in my old age. I have many regrets. It may surprise you to learn that my son is not one of them. I love that boy. It makes me proud to hear how he has dealt with your situation. A father couldn't ask for much more than that."

Abby felt her anger dissipate. "Maybe you should tell that to Kevin. Your opinion means a great deal to him."

Edward dismissed her comment with a wave of a hand. "I doubt that."

She took a seat on the sofa. "I think you'd be surprised."

"Did he really kill that man…Merrick?"

"He said he did. I have no reason not to believe him."

The man didn't look convinced.

"Kevin climbed out of a second-story window and knocked out a man twice his size who was holding a gun on me. If your son had not been there, Merrick would have killed me and not given it a second thought. Kevin saved my life."

"Never would have thought he had it in him…doing something like that. I mean, he seems more like the type to run screaming."

Sinister Winds

Abby felt her protective mode kick in. "Mr. Bishop..."

"Please call me Dad." His voice took on a plea.

She swallowed. "Dad... I married a man's man and you see how that turned out. Your son is more of a man than Jacob ever dared to be. Kevin treats me with respect, and he went above and beyond the realm of friendship. He is one of the best men I have ever met."

Edward turned his attention to a photo resting on the table beside his chair. He lifted it, studying it for some time. After several moments, he held it out to her. The photo was of a woman a bit younger than Abby, standing next to a man. At first glance, she thought the man was Kevin, but judging from the hairstyle, she knew that it was not him but a much younger version of the man sitting in front of her.

"Me and my Laura," Edward said.

"You both look very happy."

"We were," he confirmed. "But something was missing."

Abby studied the photo. "I expect that something was Kevin?"

He nodded. "She wanted a child more than anything. Once Kevin showed up, she doted on him, never letting him out of her sight."

Abby met his eyes. "Surely you don't think his mother made him gay."

He let out a chuckle. "It crossed my mind over the years. I was a cop... always on the job. I thought maybe if I'd been home more, he might have been less...different."

"Surely you don't still think the same way," she said, eyeing him critically.

He picked at some dirt under his fingernail. "No. I suppose the truth of the matter is Laura knew he was different and was trying to protect him the only way she knew how. Even at a young age, the boy wanted to wear pink shirts. I'm a cop, for Christ's sake. How was I supposed to deal with that?"

"How old was he when your wife died?"

"Twelve. Pneumonia. He had a hard time dealing with her death. He was very moody, and we had a tough time of things."

"So instead of counseling, you locked him in the closet so no one would see him?"

"I locked him in to keep him safe."

"And you a cop…"

He stopped digging at his nails and stared at her. After a moment, his glance traveled to her swollen belly. "I'd do things a lot different if given the chance."

"Meaning?"

"I took an oath to protect and serve, but in the end, I let down the two people who counted on me the most. I could not save Laura from the pneumonia that killed her any more than I could keep that boy from being gay. He loves you, Abby. Maybe not in the way that I wish he did, but he considers you family. He has done more to protect his 'family' than I ever did. I haven't told him, but I'm dying. I'm eaten up with the cancer. Damn, I wish I'd have died on the job instead of living long enough to be ravaged by this beast. I'll tell him. I just haven't found the right time."

"I'm sorry," Abby said sincerely. She smiled at the man and handed him the photo. "Kevin has forgiven you. Maybe you should try to forgive yourself."

"Do you really think he has forgiven me?"

"He told me he's learned a lot from you." She fought the urge to thank him for one particular skill. Not everyone was quite as adept at picking locks as Kevin.

Sinister Winds

The man returned the photo to its place on the table. "Kevin would make a really good dad. Are you sure you two can't be more than friends?"

Abby glanced toward the empty hallway. She had once asked herself that very question. "No, sir, not in this lifetime."

CHAPTER FOURTEEN

Abby walked into the living room and stifled a scream. Gulliver sat perched on the back of the sofa intently watching Tiffy, who was lying with her head on top of the arm of the couch, methodically pulling the stuffing out of the end of the sofa with her teeth. The dog must have been at it for quite some time, as white foam tufts littered the floor just under the armrest.

"Tiffy!" Abby scolded, causing the dog to stop and look at her in question. "I guess we know why you were in the shelter."

Unfazed by Abby's outburst, Tiffy clamped her teeth into the cushion and growled at the cat. Gulliver answered with a low feline growl but remained perched on the top of the couch as if waiting to see how Abby would handle the situation.

"Outside!" Abby said firmly.

Tiffy yawned.

"I said outside!" Abby repeated. When the dog didn't react, Abby moved to the couch, placed the dog on the floor, and repeated the command.

Tiffy lowered into a bow for a lengthy stretch, then eagerly pranced toward the kitchen as if going outside had been her idea all along. The dog stopped at the backdoor and tilted her head as if to say, *Hello, I'm waiting. Are you going to open this thing or not?*

Abby resisted rolling her eyes. "You and Kevin are made for each other."

Tiffy wagged her fluffy tail as if accepting a great compliment.

"Go on," Abby said. She opened the door and felt a blast of warm air.

Tiffy sniffed the air but didn't bother to move.

"I know it's hot, but you need to go out and do dog things. I'll be out in a minute."

Tiffy sniffed the air and trotted outside. Once in the yard, she ran along the privacy fence scattering squirrels and birds along the way. Abby watched the dog for a moment, then closed the backdoor and returned to the living room. *I should leave this mess for Kevin*, she thought, surveying the mess. *Right, it's not like you're indebted to him or anything*, she chided herself. Dropping to her knees, she went to work picking up the wayward stuffing. Several minutes later, she had crammed the stuffing back into the armrest and draped it with a hand towel. "There, good as new. Edward will never be the wiser."

Gulliver meowed and looked at her as if saying, *Yeah, right.*

"It could happen," she said, responding to the imagined comment. "That or we could convince Edward to get a new sofa before he discovers the damage."

Another meow.

She started to answer, then realized she was arguing with a cat. "Oh, Abby, you need a vacation." Besides, given the man's health, the last thing on his mind would be redecorating. He'd leave that for his son to take care of once he was no longer around to see how it turned out. Though she'd only just met him, knowing Edward was dying made her sad, especially since he hadn't yet told Kevin. While she didn't mind stepping in to help keep the peace, the last thing she wanted was for her friend to be upset at finding out she'd kept the news from him.

Gulliver meowed, bringing her from her musings.

"Yeah, I guess I should go check on the dog," Abby said, scratching the cat behind the ear. "Kevin will never forgive me if I allow her to get heat stroke."

Gulliver followed as Abby went to the back door and called to the dog. The cat attempted to stick its head out. Abby blocked his way and stuck her head out to call for the dog once more. "Tiffy!" she called as she scanned the empty yard. *Shit!* She slipped into her sandals and hurried into the yard, walking along the fence line and searching for a hole under the fence. Finding none, she went to the back and opened the gate.

"Lose something?"

Abby jumped and lifted her arm to block a blow that never came. Recovering her composure, she studied the young man who leaned casually against the fence, sizing her up. Appearing to be in his late teens or early twenties, he had twin snake tattoos on each arm that seemed to slither from beneath the sleeves of his shirt and run along each arm. The two reptiles came together just below the elbow, intertwining with one another, making the man's forearms appear menacingly alive. To add to the realism, sweat glistened off his skin, causing each movement to add life to the slithering serpents. The man's gaze drifted to her abdomen.

Abby remembered Jacob's warning and worked to

Sinister Winds

quell her fear. She took a step back, hoping to close the gate, but found she was no match for the man's strength.

Standing at least six feet tall, the guy peered down at her as he held the gate to keep it from closing. "Now, where you going, pretty momma? Snake's not here to hurt you."

"I... I'm late for an appointment," Abby said lamely. She started to turn away, and Snake stepped in front to block her escape.

"Not so fast, momma. You looked like you were looking for something," he said, smiling a toothy grin that seemed out of place given the fierceness of the ink he sported.

"My dog... I guess she ran away," Abby said, backing away from him.

The smile broadened. "Oh, that little white dog? Yeah, Snake seen him. My cousin Tawney done found that dog."

She felt her fear ebb. "You've seen my dog? Where is she?"

"Now you wait just a minute. My cousin Tawney, he's taken a liking to that dog. He's not going to want to give him up that quick." The smile left the guy's face. "Tawney be wantin' a finder's fee."

Realizing the guy wasn't there to hurt her, Abby narrowed her eyes. "That sounds like extortion."

Snake threw his hands up in the air. "Now it ain't like that, little momma. We just need to make sure that you will take good care of the dog is all. Leaving it to roam around in this heat can't be good for the little dude. As Snake said, Tawney, he really took a liking to the little fella."

"The little fella is a girl," Abby said hotly.

"Is that so?"

"Yeah, that's so. Now, how much is it going to cost me

to get the little fella back?" Abby asked, crossing her arms.

Snake smiled. "That's better. Snake knew we could come to an agreement. Now, Snake would give the dog back at no charge if he'd been the one to find it. But he didn't see, and Tawney's not as nice as me. That being the case, it'll be a fifty-dollar finder's fee."

Anger surged through her veins. "Fifty dollars?!"

"Yep, and you'd better hurry it up on account of my cousin's not a patient man. You don't agree quick, and he'll double the price."

Abby worked to keep her voice steady. "Fine. You tell Tawney to bring me the dog, and I'll get you the money."

"You bring me the money, and Snake will get you the dog," he countered.

Abby stood her ground. "No dog, no money." She turned and stomped off without waiting for him to answer. Her anger rose with every step, and she was literally fuming by the time she pulled a fifty-dollar bill from her purse and returned to the backyard to see Snake standing by the back gate. She stopped halfway, pulled out her phone, and dialed 911. "Where is my dog?"

He shrugged. "That's the thing. Snake told Tawney of your request, and he said he's the one that makes the rules."

Abby held the phone for him to see. "You tell him the rules have changed. He has two minutes to bring me my dog, or I hit send and call the cops."

Snake leaned around the fence. "Yo, Tawney, the bitch gonna call the cops on you, man." He'd no sooner said it than another young man came into view. He appeared to be around the same age as Snake but seemed less menacing since he had far fewer tattoos. He handed over the dog and stayed by the fence as Snake approached Abby.

Sinister Winds

"That's far enough," she said, dropping the bill on the ground. "Let the dog go, and you can get the money when we are in the house."

He bent and lowered the dog to the ground.

Tiffy stood looking up at him.

"Come here, Tiffy," Abby called. Tiffy trotted toward her, and Abby scooped her up with her free hand as she quickly backed toward the house. "Get the money and leave or I'll call the cops."

"Here's the thing," Snake said, smirking. "If the cops show up, me and Tawney here will know who called them. We would hate to see any harm come to the old man or the fairy who lives here. You understanding Snake's meaning, pretty momma?"

Unable to speak, Abby merely nodded.

"Good, now you go on and enjoy your day and we'll forget this ever happened." He slid the money into his pocket and turned to leave without another word.

Abby stood glued to the spot until he closed the gate behind him, and she heard laughter drift over the fence.

***

Abby stood in the kitchen, seething with anger. Fifty dollars! Fifty dollars to get a dog that was obviously stolen from the yard in the first place! She kicked at the trash can, sending the contents flying. Why couldn't she just have a normal life? Tears sprang to her eyes as she kneeled to clean up the mess she had just made.

Tiffy stepped up beside her, sniffed a soup can, and then proceeded to lick its contents. Abby took the can from her and tossed it into the receptacle. "Oh no, you don't!"

Tiffy whined and yipped at the trash bin.

"Not going to happen," Abby said. She stood and went to the cabinet to get a disinfectant wipe to clean up the remainder of the mess. When she returned, the mess was gone. She looked at the dog, who sat wagging her tail.

"Don't you try to get on my good side. I like you even less now," Abby said as she wiped the floor clean.

Tiffy leaned forward, sniffed where she'd just cleaned and sneezed.

"Serves you right," Abby said, eyeing the dog. "Some guard dog you are. You didn't even have the decency to bite the guy."

Tiffy walked to the area rug and squatted.

"Seriously?! You were just outside!" Abby pulled several more bleach wipes from the Clorox tube to clean up the urine as Tiffy sat watching her effort.

"Fifty!" Abby said, dabbing up the new mess. "Fifty dollars for a dog I didn't want in the first place." As she scrubbed, she continued to fume. Tossing the wipes, she collected her phone and went back outside. Acting braver than she felt, she walked the perimeter of the fence, looking for any possible way of escape. She found nothing, which meant there was no way Tiffy had gotten out under her own power and that the guy who had "found" her had taken her in the first place.

As she returned to the house, Abby wondered if Snake knew that Edward was a retired cop. If he did, he obviously didn't care. Oh well, she'd gotten the dog back, and no one had gotten hurt. No harm except to her already fragile sense of security.

Tiffy whined, looked at the door, and yipped.

Abby shook her head. "Oh no, you don't. I am not letting you back outside."

The comment was met with another whine and a sniff toward the damp rug.

"Don't you dare soil that rug!" Abby said, reaching for

the leash. She hooked it to the dog's collar and decided a walk would be safer than allowing the dog into the backyard. "Come on, Tiffy, we both could use a bit of exercise."

Once outside, she second-guessed her decision. Without the confines of the house or even the privacy fence, she felt vulnerable. It was the first day in the week since her arrival that she'd been left alone. Edward had gone golfing, and Kevin was out in search of computer parts. Tiffy pulled on the leash, eager to explore her new surroundings. Abby stiffened as a car eased past, did a U-turn in the cul-de-sac, and continued on its way. The mop of a security dog continued sniffing the ground, oblivious to the possible abduction. Not for the first time, she wished they'd adopted a real dog.

Abby tried to relax, telling herself that no one in their right mind would abduct a woman during the light of day, then remembered Merrick. By his own admission, he had killed Eva in broad daylight right in the heart of the French Quarter. He'd cut out her tongue and left her to bleed to death right on the street. Chills raced the length of her arms. The people who threatened her child were not normal people. They were animals who bought and sold children.

Abby tightened her grip on the leash as she forced her legs to keep moving. She had given up her freedom once. She would not be held prisoner again. She noticed a white conversion van parked along the curb on the opposite side of the street from the house, which she'd not seen before. There were no windows in the back, and the ones in front were darkened. Her first thought was to call the police, but then common sense prevailed. She was new to the neighborhood; just because she had not seen the van before did not mean it didn't belong there. She had to get a grip. Besides, how did she even know Jacob was telling the truth? Maybe he'd lied about selling the baby. She remembered his face and the matter-of-fact way he'd told her. No, he was not lying. He'd sold their child, and somewhere out there was a person or persons who would be determined to get what they'd paid for.

Abby saw a large white tree-trimming truck at the end of the street. The long mechanical arm of the truck sported a bucket, which hovered high above the street. Two workers stood inside the bucket haphazardly trimming back wayward branches. Even from a distance, Abby could tell they were working at a snail's pace, leading her to surmise they must be getting paid by the hour.

She walked along the sidewalk, watching as the crew trimmed limbs away near the power lines at the end of the lane. She crossed the street with the intention of walking around the truck, which was idling, presumably not only to power the bucket but to keep the cab of the truck cool. A good thing, because sitting in the front seat was a large Doberman pincher watching Tiffy in rapt attention. Now there was a dog that didn't miss anything. Nor did she believe it would allow itself to be taken from its own yard. Abby glanced at Tiffy and sighed. As she neared the worksite, one of the men caught her eye and nodded a greeting. Abby returned his smile, wondering at his advanced age, then glanced at the two men working in the bucket. Though she could only see their backs, both men looked to be of advanced years. *Huh, they must put all the old guys on the same work detail.*

Not trusting the guys to be able to keep the limbs from falling on them as they passed, Abby reversed her path and tugged at Tiffy's leash.

Sinister Winds

Tiffy planted herself on the curb, refusing to be pulled in the direction in which they'd just come. Abby smiled as a limb dropped to the ground several feet away, picturing the little white dog sitting unknowingly under the falling branch. Instantly, she recalled Kevin's story about using the tree branch on Merrick and shuddered.

Shaking off the image, she bent and scooped up the furry dog. "Come on, Tiffy, you may not be my favorite furry beast, but I'd rather not have to explain your demise to Kevin." After a few paces, she lowered the dog to the ground and continued walking. The dog, having no other choice, followed her down the sidewalk. As they neared the white van, she strained to see inside. It was no use. The windows were coated with a heavy tint, blocking her view. Her ears picked up a slight humming sound coming from inside. It sounded like a motor running; however, the van itself was not running. She didn't think the motor had been used anytime within the past hour as she heard no tell-tale tick of a cooling engine. Just to be sure, she placed her hand on the hood of the van. It was hot but no hotter than any other vehicle that had been left sitting in the sun on a hot Virginia morning.

Tiffy sniffed at the tires, walked to the grass, squatted to relieve herself, and then brushed at the grass with her hind legs. Making several circles, she then bunched up her haunches and further relieved herself. Abby watched in wide-eyed horror as the dog turned, sniffed the pile, and started eating what she had just left.

"Oh my God, you nasty little beast, leave that alone!" she cried out. Dragging the dog away from the smelly pile, she pulled a bag from the leash compartment and picked up the rest. They had just reached the driveway when she heard the familiar whine of Kevin's Mini Cooper. The car sped into the driveway, stopping just short of the garage door. Kevin got out, sporting a pale pink polo, and leaned casually against the car. With his short-cropped hair, sun-darkened skin, and lean dancer's body, he looked like he'd just stepped off the cover of a magazine. Leaning against the bright yellow Mini Cooper, she realized that the magazine would probably be geared toward guys. God, why in the hell did he have to be gay? Not that she ever had any intention of surrendering herself to another relationship.

"Hey, Sunshine," Kevin said as she neared. "It's good to see you outside the house."

Tiffy pulled at the leash, whimpering and straining to get to Kevin. Abby finally relented and released the leash. Tiffy ran straight to Kevin, jumping and whining to be picked up, leaving a stream of urine in her wake.

Kevin scooped her up, cooing to her as if she were a child. "Oh, you are such a good girl now, aren't you, my little muffin? Yes, you are. Yes, give Daddy kisses."

Abby cringed as the dog lapped at Kevin's face, all the while wriggling with delight.

Kevin frowned as he pulled away from the rambunctious dog. "Ugh, you have horrible breath. Just what has Mommy been feeding you?"

"Shit," Abby said, stifling a giggle.

"Shit what?" Kevin asked.

"No, Kevin, the dog eats her own shit!" Abby said and watched his tanned face go pale.

Kevin lowered the dog to the ground and made a futile attempt at wiping away the dog's greeting.

"She also likes couches," Abby added helpfully.

Kevin glanced toward the house. "How bad is it?"

Abby let loose another giggle. "Well, if she keeps it up,

your dad will have no choice but to remodel."

Kevin smiled. "Anything exciting happen around here today?"

Abby glanced at the dog, which was now lying in the driveway chewing on her leash. She wanted to tell Kevin about the dog-nappers but remembered Snake's warning. She had already lost Brian and her parents. No way was she going to put Kevin and Edward in any more danger than they were already in. Though she was out fifty dollars, she'd gotten Tiffy back, and aside from her already delicate sense of security, no one had been hurt. She smiled at Kevin and shook her head. "No, nothing much..."

CHAPTER FIFTEEN

Abby sat on the patio, watching as Tiffy sniffed her way along the fence line. Two days had passed since her encounter with Snake, and while she hated going in the backyard, she didn't feel safe letting the dog outside on her own. Since Kevin was out doing errands and Edward was hanging out golfing with friends, that left her to supervise the little stool-eater.

The ever-present sound of chainsaws drifted through the air as the tree crew continued to move leisurely up their street, removing limbs and cleaning up the tree line. The men were now a familiar sight and made a point to wave to her anytime she took Tiffy for a walk in the cul-de-sac. So much so that Abby knew she would miss their greeting when they moved on to another job.

The white van was also a staple in the neighborhood, leading her to realize it must belong to the person whose house it was parked in front of. She never mentioned its presence to Kevin or Edward as she didn't want them to think she was paranoid or needed a babysitter, even though she still jumped at every noise any time she was left alone. Thankfully, the nights were getting easier as they were filled with the sounds of the television and leisurely chatter

Sinister Winds

from Kevin and Edward, both of whom seemed content to remain home during the evening hours. While Edward had yet to tell his son of his diagnosis, the two men seemed to be on the road to healing old wounds.

Abby's pulse quickened as Tiffy lifted her head and ran to the back gate. Tail wagging, she sniffed at the gate before tilting her head upwards and letting out a high-pitched bark.

"Come here, girl," Abby said, patting her thigh.

The dog ignored her, sounding off several more yips directed at the gate. Abby watched in stunned disbelief as the gate opened on its own, and Tiffy trotted through the opening and disappeared from sight. Hoisting herself from the lounge chair, her anxiety mounted as she walked toward the back entrance. She took a breath to steady herself, then pushed the gate open.

"Here, Tiffy," Abby said softly. "Tiffy, come," she said when the dog failed to return. Abby stood listening for several moments before finally peeking to see if she could see the dog. While Tiffy wasn't there, Snake was. He reached around her and closed the gate, then peered effortlessly over the privacy fence, checking to make sure they were alone.

"I see you lost your dog again, little momma," he said, looking her up and down.

Abby flinched as he raised a hand to brush the hair from her face. She batted his hand away. "I haven't lost anything. You opened the door and let her out just like you did the first time," Abby replied, sounding much braver than she felt.

"You hurt me, momma. Snake doesn't steal. Snake's a nice guy. Snake might be inclined to show you just how nice he is, if you know what I mean." He touched her face again, lifting her chin as he drew his tongue slowly across his glistening lips.

Abby tried unsuccessfully to pull away. "You wouldn't dare," she said, narrowing her eyes at him.

He looked her up and down once more, his eyes focusing on the arch between her legs. "Oh, Snake would dare." He laughed. "Snake would do much more than dare. Snake's been thinking a lot about you. Tell me, little momma, does the carpet match the drapes?"

She firmed her jaw and fought back tears, searching her mind for a plan and wondering why neither Pearl nor Eva had warned her of this newfound threat.

Snake leaned in so that she could feel the heat of his breath. "Snake could fancy himself tasting a little milk-skinned ginger." He stroked her arm with his finger, further emphasizing the contrast of their skin tones.

Abby took a step backwards, her hand instinctively clutching the chicken's foot she kept at hand, praying its protection still worked. She attempted another step but was met with resistance from the privacy fence.

Snake smiled his triumph as he pushed against her, pressing her further into the hardened wood, his weight nearly flattening her round stomach. His breathing deepened as he lowered his head.

She was just about to scream when the baby stretched, pushing its protest against the added confinement.

Snake's eyes flew open as he released her and turned his attention to her swollen abdomen. "Whoa, that's the coolest thing ever! Did you feel that, momma? The little dude just kicked me. Does it do that often?" he asked in a fascinated tone.

Abby's mind reeled at the fact that her child just stopped an attack from inside the womb. Taking advantage

Sinister Winds

of the situation, she fought to regain control.

"Where's my dog, Snake?" she asked, somehow managing to keep the fear from sounding in her voice.

He seemed put off by her question. "Now, don't get yourself in a state, little momma. Tawney found your dog down by the end of the road."

Abby glared at him. "Then call Tawney and tell him to bring her back," she said coolly.

"Oh, he'll bring her back…just as soon as you give Snake the finder's fee."

Oh, for Pete's sake. They were treating her like their own personal cash machine. Maybe she should just let them keep the dog and solve two problems. One sight of Tiffy eating her own feces would probably ensure her safe return. Still, what if they decided to kill the pup instead? She might not be overly fond of Tiffy, but she didn't want to be the cause of her demise. "Fine, I will get the money. But this is the last time," Abby said, pulling open the gate.

"Yo, momma," Snake called after her.

Abby paused.

"Tawney's not real happy 'bout you not keeping a close eye on your dog, Tawney being so attached to her and all. He said the price is double. Said maybe that will teach you to keep a closer eye on her and all."

Abby walked through the gate and let it slam behind her.

"Is that a yes?" Snake called from the other side of the fence.

Abby was shaking as she walked away and nearly in tears by the time she reached the house. She opened the door, cursing the day she set eyes on the fluffy little dog. While she'd agreed to a dog, she'd thought they would be getting a real dog. One that would help her feel safe and protected. Not one that would literally lead her into the path of danger. Tiffy had worn out her welcome. She had enough on her plate without a couple of neighborhood hoodlums adding to her worries. She would pay the extortion money, and then, as soon as Kevin got home, she would have him drive her right to the shelter. The little shit eater could go back to her cell and wait for some other unsuspecting soul to come along and adopt her.

***

It was just past one when Kevin returned, looking as fresh and relaxed as if he'd just spent a morning at the spa. "Hey, Sunshine," he said as he approached.

Abby sat on the front porch with Tiffy, who piddled on the porch at the sound of Kevin's voice. "Don't Sunshine me," she snapped.

Kevin took a tentative step. "I see the pregnancy hormones have arrived."

"No, the pregnancy hormones have not arrived. I am sick and tired of this dog. She pees if you look at her wrong and eats everything in sight. If you want to keep her, then she is your responsibility. You go somewhere, she goes with you." She wanted to add that because of the dog, she was a hundred and fifty dollars poorer and that she'd nearly gotten raped in the process of rescuing her but didn't. This was her battle.

"What about Dad?"

Abby frowned. "What about him?"

"It was his idea to get a dog."

"She's not a dog," Abby said, willing him to understand. "Gulliver is more of a watchdog than her. At least Gulliver would hiss if he thought I was in trouble. Tiffy would open the gate and invite them in."

Kevin sat on the porch beside her. "You really don't

Sinister Winds

like her, do you?"

"Kevin, it's not about not liking her. She was supposed to help me feel safe, but I assure you that is not the case. Maybe it is pregnancy hormones, but the dog needs to go," Abby said firmly.

Kevin took Tiffy from her, holding her back enough so she could not bathe him in kisses. "I hate to admit it, but the old man was right. I guess we should have gotten a man's dog, not a girly girl."

Abby butted her shoulder against his. "Kevin, we both know the only reason you picked this dog was to goad your father."

His brows shot up. "I don't know what you are talking about."

"Like hell, you don't. You knew the second you saw her that your dad would not approve." Abby tucked her hair behind her ears. "You know he loves you, don't you?"

Kevin screwed up his mouth. "Does he?"

"He told me so himself," she assured him.

This got his attention. "When?"

"Just the other night, he told me he was proud of the man you'd become."

He laughed. "Yeah, that sounds like my pop."

"Have I ever lied to you?" she said, turning toward him.

His face brightened. "He really said that?"

"Yes." She placed her arms around her knees and debated telling him the rest of what Edward had said. In the end, she decided it wasn't her place. They sat in silence, watching the tree crew, which was working on the limbs two houses down from their house. The large truck was idling, and inside, the Doberman sat regally, watching their endeavors.

The truck engine revved slightly, and the long steel arm

propelled the bucket upward a few feet and stopped. One of the men reached for a high limb, the action exposing a snow-white gut.

"You'd think they'd be in better shape," Kevin said, sounding sorely disappointed.

"I've been thinking the same thing all week. You'd think they'd be younger," she said. "It's weird, you know."

"What's weird?" he asked, turning his attention to her.

"Guy-watching with you."

Kevin wrinkled his nose. "Sunshine, you know I love you, but you're sorely mistaken if you think I'm getting any pleasure from watching the old dudes. If you want to guy-watch, you just say the word. The beach is full of eye candy."

She shook her head. "Not interested."

"In the beach?"

"In guys. I've had my fill," she said adamantly.

"Honey, you just haven't had the right one," Kevin assured her. "Mmm, now that's more like it."

"What is?" Abby asked. She followed his gaze, stifling a gasp as Snake came out of the house across the street.

Tiffy saw him, leaped from Kevin's lap, and strained against the leash, yipping to get the guy's attention.

"See, even Tiffy likes him. Dogs know things," Kevin said approvingly.

"Tiffy doesn't know her ass from a hole in the ground," Abby said, trying to keep her voice even.

Kevin rose, extending a hand to help her up. "Okay, Sunshine, let's take Tiffy back to the clinker before you detonate."

Abby remained on the porch while Kevin went into the house to get the dog food. Snake rounded the white van and leaned casually against its side, staring in her direction.

Sinister Winds

"It looks like he's taken an interest in you. Ohhh, my, look at those tattoos. Now tell me you wouldn't like to have those arms coiled around you."

Abby shuddered at the memory of those arms snaking past her. "No, thank you," she said, following him to the car.

As Kevin started the Mini, Snake pushed off the van and started walking down the lane.

Kevin turned to her. "Why, Abigail Buckley, I didn't know you were prejudiced."

She cringed at his use of her full name.

"I am not prejudiced," she assured him. "And don't you ever say my name like that again."

"Well, that dog sure is." Kevin nodded toward the truck where the Doberman was standing in the driver's seat, watching Snake with rapt attention. As Snake neared the truck, the dog lunged at the window, teeth bared, claws digging into the sturdy glass. Snake jumped, crossed to the sidewalk on the other side of the street, and continued on his way, looking over his shoulder several times as if to assure himself the dog had not broken through the glass. Once thoroughly cleared of the truck, Snake moved back into the street and walked down the center like he owned it. Kevin attempted to drive around him, but each time, Snake shifted his position and brazenly walked in front of the Mini without so much as a backward glance.

"Oh, I guess he's entitled," Kevin said, moving the car to the other side.

Snake stepped in front of the car, once again blocking its path.

"What the heck is he doing?" Kevin said, slamming on the brakes to keep from running into the man. The game played out for several moments before Kevin finally gunned the engine, sending the car darting around the man in a near miss. Abby looked in the side mirror just in time to see Snake's toothy grin. Bile rose in her throat as she remembered her earlier encounter with the guy. She would have to find a way to stop this nonsense before it escalated. She had enough to deal with without having to worry about a teen on a power trip.

"Still think I should date a bad boy?"

"There's a difference between a bad boy and a jerk," Kevin said, maneuvering the little car down the street.

Abby closed her eyes; no, she thought, they are usually one and the same.

***

Guilt clutched at her as Kevin pulled into the shelter parking lot. It was what she wanted, what was best for everyone involved, but still, her resolve wavered when she looked into Tiffy's soft brown eyes.

"Will you take her in?" she asked, unable to do the deed.

"Not on your life, Sunshine," Kevin said, opening the door for her.

"But?" Abby pleaded.

"No buts, sister. I don't mind killing a man for you, but I'm not going to be the heavy when it comes to putting Tiffy Girl back into solitary confinement."

Abby pushed out her bottom lip. "You're mean."

"Mean? Listen, girlfriend, are you forgetting that I can feel her pain? That I know what it's like to be locked in a cage?"

"And yet you drove us here," Abby said lamely.

"Hey, don't try to lay that guilt trip on me," Kevin said, wagging a finger at her. "This is all on you. I'm not the one that can't handle a little pooch."

"She eats her own poop," Abby reminded him.

"So, she has issues. Who doesn't?" Kevin said, hoisting the bag of dog food onto his shoulder.

Abby held the leash as Tiffy jumped from the car, tail wagging. Abby sighed, knowing the dog probably wouldn't be so happy if she knew where they were going. Kevin pulled open the heavy glass door, holding it open for them to enter.

The lady at the desk looked up and gasped. "She's back!" she said, clasping her hands.

Abby hesitated, not knowing if the woman was talking about her or the dog. The answer was soon apparent as the lady rounded the desk, dropped to her knees, and greeted the dog with baby talk.

Kevin turned as if to get her take on it. Abby shrugged.

The woman stood, taking the leash. "I don't know why you brought her back, and personally, I don't care. We had a lady come in about an hour after you took her, begging us to call you. She said she had been watching Tiffy's picture on our website for days and had finally convinced her landlord to allow her to get a dog. The poor woman bawled her eyes out, pleading with us to make the call. She said the dog's eyes spoke to her." The woman retraced her steps and leafed through a pile of papers. Finding the one she was looking for, she held it up in victory.

"Found it!" she said, reaching for the phone. "If she answers, we can have Tiffy here in her new home before we close tonight."

"Should we warn her about Tiffy's fondness for poop?" Kevin whispered.

Abby kept a smile plastered on her face and kept her voice low. "Not unless you want to see the pregnancy hormones kick in."

CHAPTER SIXTEEN

Abby sat on the front porch enjoying the warm morning air while Gulliver lay just inside the door, basking in the sun. On occasion, Gulliver sounded a questioning meow as if calling out for the dog. At least, that was what it sounded like to her conscience, which still felt guilty about surrendering the dog. In reality, Gulliver's cries probably had less to do with the dog's absence and more to do with the fact that Abby was sitting outside, and he was not.

Abby thought of Tiffy and smiled. The woman at the shelter had been correct. From the moment Tiffy's new owner entered the building, it was apparent she and the dog were meant for each other. Abby was also grateful to Kevin for insisting they wait around to make sure that the dog would not have to spend the night in the shelter, as seeing Tiffy respond so well to her new owner helped ease the guilt of surrendering her. That Tiffy went to the woman without hesitation, wiggling in the woman's arms without so much as a piddle, showed the dog probably wasn't as happy in their care as they'd thought.

A door slammed, causing Abby to jump. She relaxed at seeing an older teen with long dark hair bounding down the steps of the house next door. The girl started for the sidewalk, then noticed Abby sitting on the porch and turned in her direction. While Abby had seen the girl around, they'd never spoken. Watching the girl's determined steps, Abby knew that was about to change. Seeing her up close, Abby realized she was younger than she appeared. While she initially thought the girl to be in her late teens due to her budding figure, Abby now had her pegged to be around thirteen. Abby thought about Snake and wondered if he'd ever tried his moves on the teen, a thought which infuriated her.

"You related to the old man?" the girl asked when she neared.

"Old man? You mean Mr. Bishop?" Abby said, meeting the girl's bold look.

"Yeah, Edward. He's okay for an old guy," the girl said and sat on the stoop without waiting for an invitation.

"I like him well enough," Abby agreed.

"You're not related, then." The disappointment was evident in her voice.

"No, we're not related. I'm a good friend of his son, Kevin," Abby said, wondering where the conversation was headed.

"Yeah, the one who drives the cute car. I've seen him around lately and wondered who he was." The girl took a moment to consider this. "I wonder why Edward never told me he had a son."

"He lived out of town for a long time and just moved back home a few weeks ago," Abby said by way of explanation.

"I've never seen a guy who likes to wear pink. Snake said he likes pink because he's a fag."

"What Kevin wears or does is none of Snake's business," Abby said firmly.

"Snake thinks everything on this street is his business," the girl said as she picked at a scab on her leg. "You're the one they call Ginger, right?"

Abby took a deep breath before speaking. "My name is Abby."

"Yeah, but they call you Ginger on account of you've got red hair," the girl replied.

"They?" Abby said, watching the girl dig into her leg.

The girl nodded toward the house across the street. "Snake and some of the others."

The scab loosened; blood trickled down the girl's leg. "Snake thinks he's all that. He talks a lot, but he's not being so nice when it comes to you. I'm sorry about your dog."

Abby pulled a tissue from her pocket and handed it to the girl. "What about my dog?"

The girl tore off a section of the tissue and stuck it to her leg. The paper turned crimson but succeeded in stopping the flow of blood. "Snake said he killed it to teach you a lesson."

Abby stared at the house across the street. "Snake's a liar."

The girl shrugged. "I know. If Snake didn't kill your dog, where is it?"

"We were dog-sitting and took her home," Abby said, not wanting to discuss it. She glanced at the house across the street. "Did Snake say anything else?"

The question was met by silence, yet something told her that there was more to the impromptu visit. "Please?" Abby implored. "Snake has not been very nice to me. I need to know what he's up to."

The girl looked up at Abby. "He said you ran away from your baby daddy."

Abby felt the blood drain from her face and placed her

Sinister Winds

hands across her stomach.

"Snake likes to talk," the girl said. "He said a man stopped him yesterday and said he was looking for a lady with red hair. A real ginger. Said the lady was having his baby. Told Snake he would pay him to bring you to him so you two could talk. Snake said they were negotiating the price and said he told the guy he owed you one."

The girl stood and looked toward the front door. Gulliver meowed from the other side of the glass then raised onto his hind legs and used his front paws to paw at the glass. The girl smiled for the first time since her arrival. "Edward said he used to be a cop. He could help you, ya know."

"I'm sure Snake wouldn't be happy if he found out you warned me. Why are you telling me this?" Abby asked.

The girl stood a bit taller. "I'm going to be a police officer someday. It wouldn't be right for me not to say something. Besides, I'm sure you had your reasons for leaving your baby daddy."

As the girl stepped off the porch, Abby called out to her. "Wait, what's your name?"

"My name is Patricia," she smiled a sly smile, "but my friends call me Trish."

Abby smiled a trembling smile. "Thank you, Trish."

Trish took three steps before stopping and addressing her once more. "Next time, you should get a bigger dog. Snake is scared of the big dogs."

***

Abby crossed the road in determined strides. She called Kevin's cell phone but got his voicemail. Not wanting to freak him out, she'd simply left him a message saying she was feeling a bit uneasy and asked him to come home. She figured she didn't have much time to get to Snake to find out what he knew. In her heart, she knew Jacob was dead, but she needed to get a description of the man who was looking for her, just to be sure. Even if it wasn't Jacob, she needed to know who to watch out for.

Reaching the house, she banged on Snake's door several times but got no answer. A good thing, as she was no match for the guy and would have fallen right into his hands. She took out the note from her pocket and read it to herself. *Meet me in my backyard, Ginger.* She pulled out the tape dispenser she'd found in the kitchen drawer and taped it to the door.

Okay, on to plan B, which was a decidedly smarter plan in the long run. She crossed the street and headed for the guys who were still working to clear the trees around the sidewalk just two doors down. She approached with caution, avoiding the overhead bucket and approached the guy standing near the back of the truck who had waved to her on numerous occasions. To her surprise, he looked even older up close. With white hair and sun-leathered skin, she had him pegged as being in his early seventies. How a man of that age was still doing this kind of work was impressive— even more so that the rest of the crew appeared to match him in age.

The man arched a brow and seemed surprised to see her standing there. "Morning, Lassie."

"Good morning," she said, sounding as normal as she could muster under the circumstances.

He leaned in to be heard over the sound of the tree trimmers. "Can I help you?"

Abby took a deep breath and forced a smile.

"Actually, I was hoping I could help you. You see, I've been watching you for the past couple of weeks, and I noticed that you bring your dog to work with you. It just

Sinister Winds

doesn't seem right for him to have to sit in that truck all day. I have a fenced-in yard and was wondering if maybe he could come and keep me company for a bit," she said, praying she sounded convincing.

The man took off his hat and scratched at his scalp, then tilted his head toward the bucket and cupped his hands over his mouth. "Gary, Gary!" he repeated when he received no response.

The noise from above halted, and one of the men peered over the steel rim of the bucket. "Yeah, Rob?"

"This little lady here wants to know if she can dog-sit Killer for you," he said with a chuckle.

Holy shit, the dog's name is Killer. Abby gulped, wondered if she'd lost her mind, and thought about telling the man she'd reconsidered.

The man leaning over the bucket withdrew from sight, appearing to speak with his co-worker before returning to full view. "I think that would be a dandy idea. Make sure you introduce them first and give her a run-through of his commands and hand signals."

Abby followed Rob to the truck and nearly reconsidered a second time when the enormous dog leaped from the truck. His head reached well above her waist, and she was fairly certain he would be able to look her in the eyes if he stood on his hind legs. Still, he seemed to be extremely well trained, something even more apparent as the man took the dog through a series of commands.

"Does he know any attack commands?" Abby asked and smiled a sweet smile.

Rob chuckled. "Should I be worried as to why you want the dog?"

"Oh, no," Abby said sweetly. "I just want to make sure I don't say the wrong thing."

Rob chuckled once more. "I doubt that. But just in case you find yourself in a pickle, you just give your hand a wind like you're throwing a ball and tell him to attack. Once the dog latches on, tell him to hold. Then you come find me or Gary, and we'll see to the rest."

Abby swallowed. Great, as if she hadn't caused enough trouble, she was now bringing senior citizens into the mix. Maybe she just should have asked to borrow a chainsaw instead. What was one more murder in the overall scheme of things? *Easy, Abby. I think you are on the verge of a meltdown. Crap, what if he eats Gulliver?* She stared at the dog. "How is he with cats?" Abby asked.

"He loves them as long as they don't get stuck in his throat. Relax, I'm joking. He's fine with them," Rob said upon seeing the horror that must have shown on her face.

Still questioning her sanity, Abby led the big Dobie down the street to Edward's house. Gulliver met them at the door, took one look at the dog, and sped off in the opposite direction. Killer cocked his head and followed the cat with his eyes but made no move to run after him.

"Killer, heel," Abby said. The dog slid to Abby's side and followed her to the backyard without hesitation. Once outside, she released him. Happy to be free, the dog walked the fence line, sniffing and marking his newly claimed turf. When he was finished, he stretched out beside Abby under the shade of the covered patio.

For the first time in days, Abby felt safe in the yard. Edward was right; they should have gotten a larger dog to begin with. She was contemplating her next move when Killer's head whipped up, and he emitted a long, low growl.

"Stay," she said, gesturing an open palm to the dog. Killer remained alert but stayed put as Abby crossed the

Sinister Winds

yard. She'd just reached the back gate when it opened. Snake stepped through the opening, smelling as if he'd freshly showered. He moved closer, his tall frame towering over her, causing her to question her sanity once again. The baby kicked, giving a tiny reminder of the importance of her mission. She took a deep breath to steady herself and forced a smile. "I was hoping you'd come."

"Now, see, that's more like it. It looks like the little momma has come to her senses. Snake knowed you'd been thinking of him. Thought it would only be a matter of time before you might be having second thoughts about getting yourself some brown sugar," he said, leering at her.

"I've been thinking about you a lot," Abby said, batting her eyes at him.

Snake tested the fence with his hands. "Snake thinks he'll do you right here and stick it to you until you get splinters in your ass."

"Now, Snake, we can't do it here. All those splinters wouldn't be good for the baby."

His eyes grew round. "Snake never done it with a pregnant chick before. We'd best be getting in the house, then. You are in for a treat."

"What's your hurry, Snake? You just got here. I thought we could take our time. You know, do this right," Abby told him.

"Oh, Snake will do you right, little momma," he said, grabbing his crotch.

Abby resisted the urge to laugh. "Seriously, Snake, what's your hurry? I want to take our time. I've never been with someone… like you before."

He smiled. "You mean a black dude, don't you?"

She batted her eyes once more. "You just seem so… big."

He beamed at her. "Snake's so big, you're going to wonder why you ever settled for that punk-ass baby daddy of yours."

That was the opening she'd been waiting for. "And just what do you know about my baby's daddy?"

"Snake has his ways," he said, taking hold. "Enough. Snake's done with all the talking. It's time for Snake to show you what a real man is like."

She tried to pull her arm away to give the dog the attack command but was no match for his strength. She called out as he twisted her arm behind her back and lowered his mouth to hers. She felt his tongue in her mouth, seeking out her own. She wrenched her mouth from his. "Killer, attack!" she yelled. Though she didn't include the hand signal, the dog was there in an instant, snarling as he took Snake's arm in his mouth, backing him into the fence. Abby needed the guy in one piece.

"Killer, release!" The dog let go but continued to growl. "Killer, hold!" she said, touching the dog lightly on his neck. Killer stopped growling but continued to stand guard.

"What the fuck, momma?" Snake's eyes bulged as he stared at the animal.

"What, you don't want to kidnap my friend here?" Abby said, admiring the large dog.

"Hell no, Snake don't even want to be in the same yard with the fool," he said, pressing closer to the fence.

"Good. Then tell me what I want to know, and you can go," she said.

"What do you want to know?" Snake's usually self-assured voice was shaking.

"Tell me about the man who is looking for me," she said firmly.

Sinister Winds

"How'd you know about that?" he asked without taking his eyes off the dog.

"Just tell me, Snake. I think my friend here is hungry for some brown sugar."

The dog growled, and Snake placed his free hand in front of his crotch.

"Come on, Snake, I've seen the way you strut around the street. All it's going to take is one bite, and the rooster is going to lose his cock."

"Now come on, Ginger, you can't do that. Snake needs…"

"I don't give a rat's ass what Snake needs," she said, cutting him off. "Tell me about the guy who is looking for me."

"What, was it like a one-night stand or something? You can't even remember your own baby daddy?" he said accusingly.

"Tell me, Snake."

"Don't know the guy's name. Just that he's some kind of surfer dude."

"Surfer dude?"

"Yeah, you know, long blonde hair down to his shoulders. Cracker trying to be one of the brothers."

"Brothers?"

"Yeah, dressing all gangsta and wearing his hair in some bitch-ass curls and shit," Snake said in disgust.

Abby felt her breath quicken. Pearl's words floated back to her. *No trust the stranger,* she'd said the day of Nathan Riggs' visit. Nathan was in the same business as Jacob. He wasn't here for her; he was here for her baby. Abby glared at Snake.

"You listen to me," she said through clenched teeth. "Don't you dare tell him where I am!"

This caused a chuckle. "Shit, momma, it's too late for that. He already knows. He's known for days. How do you think he found me?"

Abby felt like she was going to pass out. Of course, he knew. He wouldn't just pick a random person off the street. No way was Nathan Riggs going to get his hands on her baby. She had to think.

"Snake told you what you wanted. Now tell that dog to back off," Snake said, eyeing the Doberman.

What was she going to do with him? She hadn't planned that far ahead, but she couldn't let him go—not now. She turned to the dog. "Killer, hold," she repeated, hoping the dog would keep him there without her standing over him. She turned toward the house.

"Whoa, you ain't just going to leave me here with this dog, are you?" Snake's voice was full of panic.

"You just stay put, or the dog will tear you limb from limb," Abby said as she walked away. Her mind reeled as she approached the house. What was she going to do with Snake? How was she going to deal with Nathan? Her shoulders slumped as she realized she would have to tell Kevin and Edward. As much as she had wished to keep them out of this, it was just not possible. Mr. Jefferies. The man had said to call if she found herself in trouble. If she had trusted him in the first place, she and the baby would not be in this much of a mess. *God, Abby, how could you have been so stupid?* She reached into her pocket and dialed the number she'd programmed into the phone. Her hands trembled as the call went straight to voicemail. "Mr. Jefferies, it's Abby. Please come. I really need your help!" Her voice cracked as she rattled off Edward's address.

CHAPTER SEVENTEEN

Abby pocketed the phone as she entered the house in search of rope with which to tie Snake, and was met with Gulliver's impatient meows. "Don't worry, big guy. The dog is outside," she said as she searched the cabinets. Not finding any rope in the kitchen, she went to the garage, pulled open a drawer on the workbench, and found what she was looking for. The rope felt heavy in her hands as she climbed the steps that led to the kitchen. What on earth was she thinking? Was she expecting that Snake would just allow her to tie him up without a fight? Then again, maybe she could convince him it was a form of foreplay. Maybe so… if it wasn't for the dog. She shut the door to the garage and stifled a scream at seeing Nathan Riggs standing in the center of the kitchen brandishing a gun.

He looked at the rope and smiled a brilliant smile. "How convenient. Toss it to me, Abigail," he said, pointing his weapon at her.

"I thought you guys only take babies," Abby said, tossing him the rope.

"Mostly," he said, waving the gun. "But sometimes we get lucky with a two-for-one deal. Now, put your hands together in front of you."

She did as she was told, and winced as he wrapped the rope tightly around her wrists. "And just how do you think you are going to get me out of here? There are work crews all up and down the street."

He laughed. "You're not suggesting I should be worried about the old geezers, are you? I assure you, I am not. Besides, I have people to help me."

"You mean Snake? Look again. He is about to be lunch," she said, nodding to the backyard.

He brushed past her, peered out the door, and laughed again. "Shit, little darling, I knew you had spunk, but damn! I'm surprised you let Jacob push you around like you did."

"As you can see, it's hard to be tough when you are afraid for your life," she said dryly.

"Ah, but I offered you an out. I told you I'd take you away from all of that," he reminded her.

"I seem to remember it was part of a bet. If I'd said yes, you would have sold me out to Jacob," she said, testing the strength of the ropes.

"I would have handled Jacob, but you took care of that for me, didn't you?" He bent close and whispered in her ear, "How did it feel, Abigail? Did you enjoy draining the life right out of him? Tell me the truth, and I'll let you go."

She closed her eyes.

He moved in even closer, placing the barrel of the gun between her legs. "Did you get off on it, Abigail? Did it make you wet knowing you were hurting him the way he hurt you? Tell me, and the truth will set you free."

Nathan wasn't about to set her free, and she knew it. "You're just as sick as he was," she said, pulling away from him.

"Oh, you have no idea just how sick I can be." He eased

the steel of the gun further between her legs as the sound of chainsaws hummed in the distance.

"What now, Nathan?"

"Oh, you're supposed to call me Nate, remember? We're friends, after all."

"Do you always tie up your friends?"

He laughed. "Why hell, darling, you supplied the rope."

"Don't remind me." That gave her an idea. "Maybe we should call the dog off before he really gets hungry."

Another laugh. "Sure, you call the dog off snake boy, and then sic him on me. Nice try."

"It was worth a shot."

"I'll tell you what. We're just going to leave Skippy there to his own devices. You and I are going to take a leisurely walk across the street to that white van, and you are going to get in without causing a scene."

"The van!" If she were close to a wall, she would have beaten her head against it.

He chuckled. "I thought you had me the first day. You were suspicious but didn't have the sense to act on it. A word of advice, Abigail: Always follow your gut."

"I'll try to remember that," she said dryly. "You never told me the plan. If I'm going to follow my gut, then my gut tells me I need to know the plan."

He considered that for a moment. "Fair enough. I will take you back to my place, and we will wait for the baby to be born. Once it is born, I will deliver it to the buyer, collect the remainder of the money for the kid, and then sell you to the highest bidder. The sex slave market is ripe right now. Of course, we will have some time to ourselves between now and then." Nathan took hold of her hair, twisting it hard in his hands. His mouth hovered close to her ear, letting the words flow out hot against her skin.

That he hadn't referred to her baby as a girl let her know he was not privy to that information. She tried to pull away, but she was no match for him.

"I will have plenty of time to train you in the finer art of pleasing a man. Now, how about we take that walk before I get worked up enough to start your training right here. And just remember, slow and easy. While I don't want to kill any of the geezers, I will cut them down in a heartbeat and not lose a moment's sleep over it."

Nathan pulled her into the hallway and snatched a towel from the hall closet. He draped it over her hands to hide the fact that they were tied. "There, see, just a couple of friends heading to the beach," he said, elbowing her toward the front door.

Gulliver followed at a close clip, meowing uncontrollably. Abby was not sure if he felt the danger or if he was merely afraid the large dog would find its way back into the house.

Nathan paused at the door to address the cat. "Sorry, fellow. This is as far as you go. I don't think I could put up with all that noise on such a long ride."

Abby felt her pulse quicken. Long ride... where was he taking her? For that matter, how had he found her in the first place? "Nate," she said, trying to sound calm. "How did you find me?"

A laugh escaped him as he adjusted the towel. "It's simple actually. I lost track of you after the storm. I did a search of your house. It was easy to deduce what had happened. They hadn't found ole Jacob yet, so it was easy to get into the house and have a look around. Pity you couldn't have seen the fruit of your efforts. The man looked pretty disgusting after spending all that time in the water. Smelled even worse." His nose crinkled with disgust.

Abby watched his face with a mingle of relief and disgust as she pictured Jacob's bloated and rotting body. Her knees went weak.

Nathan tightened his hold on her. Pulling her up, he opened the door and guided her onto the porch. "Now we are going to walk to the van, nice and easy like. Just like I said. A happy couple on their way out for a drive."

She glanced at the tree crew working on the other side of the street and considered calling out to them.

"Don't even think of it. Unless...you get your kicks out of seeing people die." He removed the gun he'd held at the small of her back. Resting it on her shoulder, he took aim at one of the old men in the bucket. "It would be so easy. Click, click, click, three dead old guys. What do you say, Abby? Do you think I should put them out of their misery? Surely they don't like going to work every day at their advanced age. We'd probably be doing them all a favor."

She swallowed, remembering the kindness of the men only moments before. It dawned on her they might wonder what she'd done with the dog.

"No! No," she said more calmly. "Please leave them be...I will go with you."

"Good girl," he said, lowering the gun. "Now we will walk to the van and chat as if everything is just dandy."

She nodded her agreement and they started across the street. Nathan looped his arm through hers, keeping her close.

"Searching the house could not have led you here," Abby said, picking up the earlier discussion.

"No, your boyfriend did. You see, I was looking out the window and saw a body. Turned out it belonged to

Merrick. You'd have thought all that water would have washed him away, wouldn't you? Lucky for me, his body got caught up in the bushes." Nathan led her around to the passenger's side and opened the door. "You and your boyfriend are not really very good at this, are you? You're supposed to get rid of the bodies after you do away with them."

"I'll try to remember that in the future," she said, sliding into the seat.

"After I realized you two were in cahoots, it didn't take much digging to find out where his old man lived. I took a chance that you'd be joining him. People are so predictable." He held the gun on her as he fastened the seat belt across her tethered arms.

"Smile."

"What?"

"One of the old dudes is looking this way. I want you to smile so he can see everything is okay."

She did as she was told.

"Okay, now kiss me," he said, his eyes twinkling.

"Not on your life!" she said, narrowing her eyes.

He looked past her, bringing the gun up. "What about on theirs?"

"You're a sadist," she said, faking a smile.

"Baby, you have no idea. Oh, and in case you are planning your escape, I just thought you should know that I called the cops after I left New Orleans. I told them where to find Jacob's body and let them know I'd witnessed some marital troubles between you and your husband. I told them I figured you killed the man and used the storm as a cover."

She felt the blood drain from her face as the gravity of her situation hit her and realized she had no proof to the

Sinister Winds

contrary. She would end up in jail, and the baby would be taken away. Any scenario she played in her mind ended the same. It appeared she and her baby were destined to be separated. Nathan leaned in and kissed her. She just sat there, numb, not offering to kiss him back.

"I can see we really do need to work on your man-pleasing techniques. If you treat your future owner like that, he will demand his money back. I have a reputation to uphold," he said before closing the door.

She watched helplessly as he walked around the front of the van, opened the driver's side door, and got in. He slipped the keys into the ignition and started the van, placing it into gear.

"You know the rules, Darling," he said, easing his foot off the brake.

His words sent a chill along her spine. He sounded so much like Jacob that she panicked, screaming and fighting against her restraints. The van surged forward, causing one of the tree guys to jump out of the way. Suddenly, a loud thump hit the roof. Nathan slammed on the brakes, sending a body tumbling over the windshield and onto the hood. Abby screamed, "Edward!"

Edward held on to the wiper blades in a struggle to keep from falling to the ground.

A sadistic smile played across Nathan's face as he calmly placed the van into park, opened the door, and fired.

Abby screamed as Edward sank down the length of the hood, disappearing from sight. Nathan turned and pointed the pistol in her direction. A loud gunshot pierced the air, sending Nathan backward. His gun discharged as he fell, shattering the window beside her. Abby screamed as her door jerked open.

"It's okay, Abby," the man said as he hurried to

unbuckle her seatbelt and used a blade to cut the ropes. She now recognized the man as Gary, one of the men from the bucket truck. The bucket! She remembered the sound on the roof just before Edward slid into sight. Edward had been the second man in the bucket of the truck. The one who had always kept his face from view. The one who had leaped from his perch to save her.

"Edward!" she said, pushing her way past Gary and rounding the van. She found him lying in front of the van with a gunshot wound to the chest.

Soaked in blood, he struggled to breathe. "I saved you, Little Missy, didn't I?"

Sinking to the ground, she placed his head on her lap. "Yes, you did," she sobbed.

Gary returned to the van, reappearing a moment later, handing her the towel, which she pressed into the wound.

The third man, Rob, the one who had loaned her the dog, appeared into view with Nathan, who was cuffed and bleeding from the shoulder.

Nathan groaned as the man tugged on the cuffs without any regard for his wound. He emitted a wicked laugh as they began to lead him away and then glared at Abby.

"I assure you it's far from over. There are others, you know! They will come for you! You will never be safe. Your child is marked. Your child will never be yours!" he cried out as he was led away.

Abby cradled Edward's head in her lap, pressing the towel to his chest as he struggled for air.

"Are you still there, girl?" Edward said between gasps.

"I'm here, Edward," she said, sobbing. She heard the familiar whine of the Mini Cooper and watched as the car slid to a stop. Kevin took in the situation as he raced toward them.

Sinister Winds

"You tell my son I saved you. Will you?" Edward said between breaths. "You tell him I am proud of him." Edward closed his eyes as Kevin reached them.

Keven sank beside her and pulled his father close. "I'm here, Pop. You tell me yourself."

Edward opened his eyes and forced a smile. "I've made so many mistakes in my life, but you were never one of them."

"I love you, Dad," Kevin said. Tears streamed down his face as he clutched his father to his chest.

"I love you too, son. I nearly missed the chance to tell you how proud I am of you," Edward said through wheezing breaths.

"Hang on, Dad, help will be here soon," Kevin pleaded.

"Abby, are you still here, girl?" Edward asked, groping the ground with his free hand.

"I'm here, Dad," she said, clasping the hand.

"You take care of my son. He needs a strong woman in his life whether he realizes it or not."

"I'll always be here for him," she promised.

"Kevin?" The name came out in a whisper.

"I'm still here, Dad," Kevin said, leaning closer.

"You take care of Abby too. She needs a strong man."

"I will, Pop," Kevin promised.

"Don't cry, son. This is a good day; I always wanted to die on the job." Edward took one final breath, and the blood-stained towel stood perfectly still.

***

Abby was not sure how long they'd sat there, her holding on to Edward's hand, Kevin lying on the ground next to him, both keeping him company until they were peeled away from his blood-soaked body. It was only when she'd been led to the house that she realized the house was now crammed with people. She was guided to the sofa, which she gratefully accepted. Gulliver jumped onto her lap and sniffed her with disdain before hissing and scurrying away. It was only then that she realized she herself was covered in Edward's blood.

"I killed him," she said, staring at her hands.

"You killed who?"

She looked toward the voice and saw a woman with blonde hair sitting across from her. Abby frowned. "Do I know you?"

The woman flashed a badge and then held her pen, ready to jot down anything Abby said. "My name is Detective Remmy. We met when they brought you inside a few moments ago. You were telling me what happened."

Abby looked out the window, watching Kevin, who hovered near his father, while paramedics loaded the man onto a gurney. Kevin dropped to his knees as the paramedic pulled the sheet across his father's prone body. Abby started to rise and felt a hand on her shoulder.

"He will be okay." The woman's words floated around her like a fog.

Abby blinked, not comprehending. "What?"

"I'm sorry, but I need to ask you some questions," Detective Remmy said firmly. "You said you killed him? Are you talking about your husband?"

"No, Edward. I didn't pull the trigger, but he is dead because of me," Abby said.

The detective jotted something on the paper. "Could you elaborate?"

Abby heard the dog bark. "The dog has someone in the backyard," Abby said, getting up. She walked to the back window and looked out to see Rob and Gary standing beside two uniformed officers. Gary was holding tight to

Sinister Winds

Killer's leash as Snake gestured wildly in the direction of the house.

"Why did the tree guys have guns?" Abby asked.

"They were friends of Mr. Bishop. They all retired from the force a long time ago. Apparently, they were all doing surveillance, posing as tree guys to get a better view of the house."

"Edward was the third guy. He jumped onto the van to save me," Abby said, turning to her.

"Yes, Mr. Bishop was also involved in the stakeout," Detective Remmy confirmed.

"They saved my life," Abby said, choking up.

"Your friend doesn't look too happy," Detective Remmy said, peering out the window.

Abby followed her gaze. The detective was right. Snake looked even more agitated than before.

"He doesn't like big dogs," Abby replied. She reached to wipe her face, saw the blood on her hands, and moved to the sink. Turning on the water, she picked up the bar of soap and thrust her hands under the stream. "I should have gotten a big dog."

Detective Remmy moved up beside her. "Excuse me?"

"Snake doesn't like big dogs," she repeated.

"So it appears," the woman said, staring out the window.

"If I'd have gotten a big dog, then maybe Edward would still be alive." Abby pulled her hands from the sink and examined them. Satisfied, she pulled the towel from the hook and dried her arms. Then, seeing her shirt, she stuck the towel under the faucet and then wrung it out before making a futile attempt at removing the blood from her blouse. Unable to clean the shirt, she tossed the towel in the sink and went back to the table, lowering herself into her chair. "They say the baby can hear what goes on around it even while it is in the womb. Do you think that's true?"

Detective Remmy joined her at the table. "There is enough craziness for children to have to deal with after they're born. I would like to think a baby is protected while in the womb."

Abby reached into her pocket and pulled out the chicken's foot. She studied it, relieved that the blood had not penetrated the talon. "Pearl told me my child would be born with protection."

Detective Remmy watched her with interest. "Pearl?"

"She was the voodoo priestess I met in New Orleans after my husband had her sister killed."

Detective Remmy's eyes grew round. "Mrs. Buckley, I think we should finish this conversation down at the station."

CHAPTER EIGHTEEN

As Abby looked around the small room, the walls felt as if they were closing in on her. She'd never been claustrophobic before, but then, she'd never been in an interrogation room either. She shifted in her seat for the hundredth time, trying unsuccessfully to find a comfortable position in the hard plastic chair. She'd watched enough television to know she was being watched. Her gaze came to rest on the large mirror, the only decoration in the otherwise sterile room.

Show yourselves! she willed, peering at the glass. Her silent demand went unanswered, and she tore her gaze from the glass. A sudden urge to extend her arms to see if she could touch the walls struck her. This was nothing like the inquisition rooms they showed on TV. There was no table. No clock so she could gauge how much time had passed. Just a room, a mirror, and two chairs. One chair was padded and looked rather comfortable. The other, the one she'd been assigned, was hard, without so much as a chair cushion. She contemplated moving to the padded chair, figuring whoever was watching her would not want her to get too comfortable; therefore, doing so would probably move things along. Not only was she ready to get this over with, but she also desperately had to pee.

She had been in the room for what seemed like hours, speaking with Detective Remmy and answering the same questions over and over. It was amazing how many ways one could ask the same question. At least the detective saw fit to read Abby her rights on the way to the station.

The baby kicked, reminding her of the seriousness of her situation as a vision of giving birth in a prison cell came to mind, sending a chill down her spine. She looked about the room once more, her heartbeat increasing as she realized the room she now found uncomfortably small was probably larger than the prison cell she'd likely spend the rest of her days in. The baby stretched against her bladder. Abby adjusted in her seat once more and placed her hands on her abdomen to comfort both herself and her unborn child. Another kick greeted her embrace. *What am I going to do with you, little one?* The thought pulled at her heart. Moms were supposed to protect their children. She wondered if there were programs that would allow her to keep her child with her in prison. Probably not, or women in similar circumstances would be more likely to commit crimes to evade their abuser. She couldn't let her daughter go into the system. According to both Jacob and Nathan, there were others out there with their sights on her daughter. If her baby were to go into foster care, it was only a matter of time before they found her.

Kevin. He said he would give his life to protect the baby. Would he still feel that way if she wasn't around to help with the baby's care? Would he even agree, now that she had literally led a killer to his door? She recalled Kevin sitting in the street crying while his father died in his arms. How could she ask him to raise her baby, knowing she was the reason for his father's death? *Because you have no other choice.*

The baby stretched, and she thought of Pearl. Her hand instinctively went in search of the chicken foot, then she remembered someone had taken it from her when they searched her before leading her to the room. She tugged at the bloody shirt she had on, wishing they had taken that as well. Then she thought of Mr. Jefferies and wondered if he'd ever gotten her message. If she'd only been forthcoming with him in the first place...

The door opened, startling her. A man she'd not seen before entered the room carrying a manila file folder that she had no doubt held the evidence that would seal her fate. The door clicked shut as he took the empty seat across from her. She thought about asking for an attorney but knew the attention of a long, drawn-out trial would bring in the press and lead to stories that would attract the attention of those looking to come for her child. Though they might find her daughter eventually, she would do nothing to make it easy for them. Abby steadied herself, wondering if she should save him the trouble and just admit to murdering her husband. Her eyes cut to the mirror, and she wondered who was on the other side. She opened her mouth to ask but thought better of it. She'd come this far; maybe she should just hear what the man had to say.

The newcomer leaned back in his chair, crossed his legs, and let the file rest on his lap unopened. "Mrs. Buckley, I'm Detective Kyle Rivers. Do you know why we have you here?"

Abby sighed, knowing the guy was probably Detective Remmy's partner stepping in to ask the same questions she'd just answered. She searched the man's face and wondered if he was supposed to be the good cop or the bad cop. Either way, he didn't look like much of a threat. With dark hair clipped so short there was no need for a comb, large brown owl eyes filled with excitement, and a boyish face not yet hardened from years on the job, he looked more like a Sunday school teacher. On one hand, she was pleased they'd sent a baby to interrogate her. On the other hand, his lack of a smile gave her pause. Wrapping her arms even tighter around her abdomen, she shook her head. "No, sir," she lied.

"You were pulled from your rooftop after Hurricane Katrina. Is that correct?" he said solemnly.

"That is correct," she confirmed, answering a question that had already been asked and acknowledged multiple times since being in the room.

"Where were you taken?"

"To the airport in New Orleans. Later, they took me to Mississippi, where I spent nearly two weeks in the hospital treated for extreme dehydration and early labor," she added, then chided herself for giving more information than was asked for.

He glanced at her abdomen. "I trust everything is okay in that department?"

"Yes, my baby is fine," Abby said, limiting her answer.

Rivers' face remained stoic. "It says here you made an outside call while you were in the hospital."

"I had to let a friend know I was safe," she said, meeting his stare.

He opened the folder and glanced at the contents. "Your friend... that would be Kevin Bishop, whose house you have been staying in since you arrived in Virginia, correct?"

"It was his father's house," Abby said, pulling at her shirt once more.

"Kevin was your neighbor in New Orleans, was he

Sinister Winds

not?"

Abby nodded.

"Please answer using words," Rivers told her.

"That's right," Abby said firmly.

"Are you and Mr. Bishop romantically involved?" Rivers asked, closing the folder.

She giggled.

"Your words, Mrs. Buckley, and I assure you there is nothing funny about your current situation."

"I'm sorry, it's just…well…have you ever met Kevin?" she asked.

"No, I haven't had the pleasure," Rivers said.

"Oh, I assure you the pleasure will be all his. Mr. Rivers, Kevin is gay."

"I see." A blush crept up the man's face as his eyes darted to the mirror. Abby wondered if it was because she'd embarrassed him or if whoever was listening had not bothered to mention that to him before he came into the room. "So, you did not murder your husband so the two of you could be together?" Rivers asked, regaining his composure.

"My husband drowned in the flood," she said pointedly.

"Please answer my question."

"No."

"No, you're not answering?"

"No, I did not murder my husband, and no, Kevin and I are not lovers," Abby informed him.

"Not yet?"

"Not in this lifetime," Abby said, leaving little room for further questions on the subject.

"You said your husband drowned."

"He did."

"Yet, somehow you managed to get out. How convenient." His eyes were fixed on hers, gauging her reaction.

"Would you have preferred I drown with him?" Abby asked. His gaze traveled the length of her arms as if searching for something. She steadied herself, fighting the urge to shield herself against his stare. The bruises were gone, but she knew that was the evidence he was looking for.

"Your husband beat you over and over from your own admission. You're saying a man could do that to you, and you did not wish to cause him harm?"

"Mr. Rivers, my husband drowned," she repeated. Better to stick to the truth and admit nothing.

"Your husband had a record and was known for his violent outbursts. It's understandable for a woman to get angry. Especially a woman who has a child to protect," Rivers said, eyeing her stomach.

Jacob had a record? She'd known him all her life and had never heard…Mr. Jefferies would have told her if Jacob had a record. Abby realized Rivers was playing her. She worked to keep her voice steady. "My husband is dead. What happened between us died with him."

Rivers uncrossed his legs and leaned in closer. "Mrs. Buckley, would you happen to know anything about the bullet holes found in your husband's office?"

She'd forgotten the gun during her escape, but it wasn't her gun; it was Merrick's. Surely her fingerprints would have been washed away during the flood. She shrugged. "You said it yourself, Mr. Rivers, my husband had quite the temper. I'm sure if they were thorough, they also found a bullet hole in the bedroom. Just another day at Buckley Manor."

His lips spread with a hint of a smile. "Yet you had no reason to kill the man?"

She met his stare. "Mr. Rivers, did you find a bullet hole in my husband?"

He shook his head. "We did not."

"Did you find any sign of trauma that would lead you to believe I killed my husband?"

"The autopsy reports state that Jacob Buckley drowned," he said in answer to her question.

Not able to stop herself, Abby continued. "Were you in New Orleans during the hurricane?"

The barest hint of a smile played on the man's lips. "I was not."

"Did you at least watch it on the news?" Abby asked.

"Of course I did," Rivers replied.

"Then you know there were many unfortunate deaths in the wake of Hurricane Katrina. My husband just happened to be one of them. I'm tired of all these questions. Tired of being made to feel guilty that I survived," Abby said wearily.

Rivers opened the folder and produced a picture, holding it out for her to see. "Do you recognize this trunk?"

A chill slid through her and she fought the urge to rub her arms. "Yes, I do."

"There were marks on the floor to suggest that someone pushed the trunk over the opening to perhaps prevent someone from following. There are bullet holes in the ceiling to suggest that someone was not pleased about that," he said, keeping the photo in her field of vision.

"Detective Rivers, look at me. I'm five-foot-three, pregnant, and was severely dehydrated at the time of the hurricane. How in heaven's name do you think I could have moved that trunk on my own?" She paused, hoping he had an answer because she'd asked herself that same question many times.

"Do you know what was in that trunk?" Detective Rivers asked, lowering the photo and changing his tactic.

Her head jerked up. What on earth did the contents of the trunk have to do with the fact that she'd used it to kill her husband? She shook her head.

"Remember, we are supposed to use our words, Mrs. Buckley," he said in a condescending tone.

"No."

"Allow me to repeat the question. Do you know what was in that trunk?" he said, speaking to her as if she were a child and placing emphasis on each word.

She'd heard the question. She just didn't understand the relevance. She suddenly wondered at the contents. Contents so bad even Kevin hadn't told her what he'd seen, at least she didn't think he had. She searched her mind, trying to recall if he'd ever said anything. If he had, she couldn't recall him doing so. "No, the trunk was always locked."

Rivers stared at her for several seconds. She wasn't sure if he was searching his mind for his next question or hoping she'd reconsider her answer. "But you do recognize the trunk as belonging to you?"

"No," Abby replied.

"Mrs. Buckley, you stated the opposite a few moments ago," he reminded her.

"No, I said I recognized it. The trunk does not belong to me. It is my husband's. Was," she said, correcting herself.

"You're going to tell me the trunk was in your house, and you never got curious enough to open it and see what was inside?" He showed her the photo once more, holding it in front of her face for several moments as if doing so would jar her memory.

She stared at the picture without answering.

"Mrs. Buckley, I asked if you ever opened the trunk to see what was inside." Rivers' voice was tight.

"You can keep me here all night and keep rephrasing the question any way you'd like, but I have never seen inside that trunk," Abby said truthfully.

Rivers shoved the photo back in the folder and stood so abruptly that his chair scooted backward. He cocked his head, stared at her intently, then left the room without another word.

Abby shifted in her seat, wondering how long they had searched to find the perfect chairs which would elicit a fast confession. She cast a glance at the mirror, wondering what was going on in the other room. She thought once again about switching to the other chair and had just made up her mind to do so when the door opened.

Rivers came into the room, wielding two paper coffee cups, and offered her one.

Abby shook her head. "No, thank you."

"You don't care for coffee?" He seemed surprised.

"Mr. Rivers, you've never been around a pregnant woman, have you? I've been in this room for several hours, sitting on probably the world's most uncomfortable chair. If I were to drink anything at this point, I would not be able to hold my bladder long enough to make it to the bathroom," she said irritably.

To his credit, he actually looked concerned. "No one has allowed you a bathroom break?"

"Once. But that doesn't matter. I'm pregnant, remember? I had to go within five minutes of returning to our little cubicle." She stopped short of telling him she was ready to confess to murder just so she could empty her bladder, take a shower, and change into an orange jumpsuit, just so she could be rid of the blood and go lie on a cot in her cell.

The door clicked open and Detective Remmy stuck her head inside.

Rivers looked up to see who had entered. "Detective Remmy?"

His partner. Abby sighed as the blonde entered the room. This must be where they start the good cop, bad cop routine.

Detective Remmy smiled. "Ready for a bathroom break?"

Oh, thank goodness, she must have heard my comment through the two-way mirror. Hoisting herself out of the chair, Abby followed her down the hall, admiring the woman's slim figure. It had been months since she'd seen her own waist. She started to say as much, but the woman hadn't spoken to her other than asking if she had to go to the restroom, and she didn't want to open the door to another barrage of questions. She'd seen enough television shows to know the woman was probably a plant, waiting for Abby to open up about her unfair detainment. No way she was going to fall for that. Unless Remmy started the conversation, she would keep her mouth shut; even then, she would choose her words wisely.

Once inside the bathroom stall, she locked the door and leaned against the wall, enjoying the brief reprieve. If her hunch about going to prison was right, it could be her last moment of privacy. While she wasn't truly alone, there were no mirrors watching. She used the bathroom, enjoying the relief of having emptied her bladder. Unable to shake the memory of Edward's blood, she took her time washing her hands.

"Feel better?" Detective Remmy asked.

Abby rubbed at the small of her back. "Parts of me do," Abby said and headed for the door. The woman reached around her and opened the door. There were no further questions as they walked back to the room.

"Take the other seat if you please, Mrs. Buckley," Rivers said when she entered the room alone.

Abby sighed as she sank onto the comfy cushion. Rivers sat in the hard chair and shifted several times. Not finding a position that suited him, he rose and proceeded to pace the room.

"Mrs. Buckley, were you aware of what your husband did for a living?" he asked, resuming the earlier line of questioning.

"Not entirely."

"Would you care to elaborate?" he said.

"I had thought maybe he was into drugs or with the mob."

"You thought this before you agreed to marry him?"

"Of course not." Even though Abby was sure he'd been listening in while she was talking to Detective Remmy, she repeated what she had told the woman about what Kevin had found on the computer. Unable to stop herself, she told about the clippings they'd found in the album and her suspicions regarding her own abduction. She told him about Brian and her "adoptive" parents and everything else she knew while leaving out that Merrick had caught them snooping or that Kevin had hit him with the lamp.

Rivers sat in the chair once more and listened intently as she spoke. Every now and again, he shifted in his seat. "So you found all this out just before your husband's death, and yet you insist you had nothing to do with the man's death?"

How many more times would he insist on asking her that? *Seriously, either arrest me or let me go, but stop with the damn questioning.* Abby sighed. "Mr. Rivers, I assure you that while I might wish I had never met my husband and wished him dead many times since our wedding day, I did not kill him."

Rivers stood. "That's right, he drowned. But why was that, Mrs. Buckley? How was it you were able to get up into the attic, but your husband couldn't?"

Something inside her snapped, and suddenly, she couldn't take it anymore. She was tired of being in a room without windows. Tired of her bladder, which was once again feeling full, and tired of the cat and mouse games, which at this point might or might not get her sent to prison. "Because I couldn't pull the damn trigger!" she screamed. "I had the gun pointed at him. I wanted to shoot him for all he'd put me through, but I couldn't follow through with it. My husband actually smiled while admitting to killing everyone I have ever loved. He'd just confessed to selling our child and told me there was not a damn thing I could do about it, and yet I couldn't put a friggin bullet in his skull!"

The door clicked open, interrupting her confession as Detective Remmy entered and handed her a handful of tissues. Abby wiped the tears from her eyes, not knowing when they had begun.

"I think we've heard enough, Mrs. Buckley. The autopsy said your husband drowned. Why don't we just leave it at that," she said softly. "Go to the bathroom and compose yourself."

Abby blinked her confusion. "You believe me? Does that mean I can go?"

Sinister Winds

The woman glanced at the mirror. "There are still a couple of things we need to clarify, but it shouldn't be much longer."

CHAPTER NINETEEN

Abby opened the door to the interrogation room, saw Belinda Winters standing in the center of the room, and froze. For a moment, she found herself wondering if they'd brought Belinda in to testify to what she had told her on the plane, a thought that was quickly dispelled when Belinda pulled the edge of her suit coat back to reveal a badge.

Belinda smiled. "Hello, Abigail. How are you holding up?"

Abby narrowed her eyes at the woman. "You're a cop?"

"FBI," Belinda clarified.

"All those questions?" Abby searched her mind for anything she might have said.

"Were answered the same as they were today," she replied.

"So, you lied to me," Abby said. "All that concern and showing me how to get to my gate. Is your name really even Belinda?"

"Yes, that is my name, although here, they call me Agent Winters. Sit; we'll both be more comfortable," she said, pointing to the chairs.

Sinister Winds

Abby turned to see a third chair had been brought into the room. She sat and waited for Belinda to join her. "Do you really believe me or is this just another of your tricks to try and get me to change my story?"

"It's not a trick." Belinda glanced toward the mirror. "We believe that your husband drowned."

"But?"

Belinda held her stare for a solid minute then lowered her eyes to scan the outlines of Abby's unseen bruises. Bruises that had still been somewhat visible when they'd last met. When done, Belinda pushed off the chair and stood facing the mirror. "Mrs. Buckley, you have been through a great deal. Your husband's death must be very upsetting." Belinda turned to her. "Your husband's death was a tragic accident. There is no need to ever relive it."

Abby was stunned. "You mean?"

"I mean your husband was an evil man. Between what we found in the trunk and on the attic computer, there is not a jury in the country that would convict you. Hell, they'd name a street after you if they thought for a moment that you'd helped rid the world of such an awful man. Now, don't you think it would be best to save the taxpayers' money and let the man drown?"

"He did drown," Abby reminded her.

Belinda lowered her voice to a whisper. "Yes, but we both know the water had a bit of help taking him."

Abby stared at her wide-eyed, admitting nothing.

Belinda kept her voice low. "You did what you had to do to survive, Abigail. I would have done the same if in your shoes." Belinda moved about the room and spoke in a normal tone. "The autopsy states the cause of death as drowning. Other than the damage from being underwater for an extended period of time, there is no evidence of foul play on your part. I think it is safe to assume the scratches we found on the attic floor were made by your husband, who, on occasion, moved the trunk over the opening to keep you from bothering him."

The relief washed over Abby like a wave as a new onset of tears trickled down her face. "Then why put me through all of this if you were going to let me go?"

"We had to make sure you were not a willing accomplice."

Abby laughed through her tears. "You mean you thought there was a chance that I enjoyed serving as my husband's punching bag?"

Belinda shrugged. "You'd be surprised what people get off on."

"I am not one of those people." Abby sniffed and thought of all the things Jacob had done to her, how he'd controlled the narrative of her life up until this very moment, and what he'd done to those she cared for. "So, after everything he did, Jacob gets off scot-free?"

"You mean besides being dead?" Belinda reminded her. "The investigation is far from over. We believe Jacob to have been the mastermind of the operation, but there are others out there who have either taken his place or are in a war to see who ends up on top. Thanks to you, we have two of the top tiers."

"Jacob told me he sold our child," Abby said. "He said it wouldn't matter if he were dead or not, that they would find me and take my child away. I thought maybe he was just trying to scare me, but now I know it to be true."

"That's why Nathan Riggs was at the house," Belinda said.

"Yes, but it's not just him," Abby said. "Jacob told me our baby would never be mine. He said I can't protect her."

Sinister Winds

"Let's stick with Nathan for a moment. He followed you to Virginia. Did he say how?"

Abby searched her mind, trying to figure out a way to answer without incriminating Kevin. She pictured Edward's body and burst into tears, knowing she was responsible for his death. "It's all my fault! Nathan wouldn't have been there if not for me. Edward is dead, and it's all my fault."

"According to his son, Edward was eaten up with cancer. He said the man died a righteous death and a better one than he'd previously been facing."

Abby couldn't believe her ears. "Kevin knew about his father's cancer?"

Belinda nodded. "Apparently so."

"You talked to him? Is he okay?"

"He's holding up," Belinda replied, then waited for Abby's tears to run their course. "I've spoken to some who knew Mr. Bishop. They all said Edward was a good man."

Abby nodded.

Belinda sat in the chair once more. "Let's circle back to Nathan Riggs. What do you know about him?"

"He came to our house once. I've already told everyone all I know. You have him in custody; if you want to know anything else, you're going to have to ask him," Abby said, frustrated by the fact that she needed to keep repeating herself.

"We found some e-mail exchanges on your husband's computer. It seems as if one of his clients was the highest bidder, but we do not have the name of that client, just an ID number. We've asked Riggs who the number belongs to, but the man claims he doesn't know. He says they each have their own system, which they do not share. That way, if one gets caught, they can't use the information to broker a deal."

"Can't you force him to talk?" Abby asked.

"I'm afraid not. Sometimes we can offer deals… but he'd ask for immunity, and the agency doesn't like to cut deals with animals who do things like that to children."

Abby felt the color drain from her face. Though both Jacob and Nathan had told her there would be others coming for her child, a part of her had hoped it was just them trying to instill fear. Now she knew the truth, that while she managed to free herself from Jacob, both the man and his plan to control every aspect of her life would continue to haunt her well beyond the grave. She looked at Belinda, praying the woman would quell her fears. "Nate told me there'd be others. This isn't over, is it?"

Belinda shook her head. "Unfortunately, not. It appears this is just the tip of the iceberg. Child trafficking is a growing crime in the US. There are numerous cells and networks. Normally, with a crime, all you have to do is to cut off the head of the snake, but in something like this, the next snake slithers into place and takes over."

Abby blew out a jagged breath. How was she supposed to keep her baby safe when she didn't know who was after her? She wrapped her arms around her stomach. "So, now what?" she asked, echoing her inner thoughts.

"Now, we get you into protective custody before the nest gets stirred," Belinda said.

"Protective custody?" Abby repeated. "Like a safe house?"

Belinda stood and walked to the mirror. "You want to weigh in here?"

A moment later, the door opened, and Alfred Jefferies walked into the room wearing a dark suit that looked as if it had been slept in. "Hello, Abby. It's good to see you again."

Abby frowned at the man. "You've been here all along?"

"About an hour. I was in the field and hopped a jet the moment I checked my voicemail." Jefferies nodded to Belinda. "See to it we don't have an audience, and then go take care of that other thing."

Abby waited until the woman left and waved her hand to encompass the room. "You mean this was all you?"

Jefferies shook his head. "No, Agent Winters is with me; we just commandeered your case from the detectives. Seems you said something that caused them to bring you in and also caused someone to check in with the authorities in New Orleans, who informed them they'd gotten an anonymous tip saying you killed your husband and covered it up with the storm. The tipster also implicated your boyfriend."

Kevin! And after all she'd done to keep his name out of this. *Damn you, Nathan Riggs!* "The informant was Nathan Riggs. He told me so himself. And I've told you, Kevin is just a friend," Abby said heatedly.

Jefferies held up his hand. "Take it easy. I didn't say anyone believed the caller, but once it came to their attention, they had to follow up on it. I didn't know anyone had brought you in until we got to the house."

"You said you've been here an hour. Why didn't you come in?"

"I was waiting until I got official word I could step in. There are channels." He smiled. "I watched what I could and glanced over the notes. You did well, Abby. You stuck to the facts."

"So, what now? I get a sticker and a lollypop?"

"Those things can be arranged if you want. I was

thinking about something a bit more long-term."

"Yeah, like a safe house. Belinda told me. Only what happens then? I sit in a hotel room forever, waiting for someone to finally tell me it's safe to go home. We both know it will never be safe."

"And that's precisely why I don't recommend you going to a safe house," Jefferies said.

Abby felt the panic rise. While she didn't like the idea, she didn't want to be left on her own either. She'd tried that method, and it hadn't turned out so well. "But Belinda said…"

"Belinda doesn't get visits from the spirit of a Cajun woman telling her she needs to protect you," Jefferies said, cutting her off.

Abby blinked in her surprise. "Eva visited you. Again?"

Jefferies looked to the mirror and lowered his voice. "Three times now. I had my doubts after the first time, but she knew about them finding the body in your friend's backyard even before I found out."

"Nathan told me he saw Merrick in Kevin's backyard, but I didn't know if he was serious." She lowered her voice to match his. "I didn't tell them about him."

"They already know."

Abby frowned. "They didn't mention him."

"They would have if I hadn't sent Belinda in when I did."

"I need to warn Kevin."

"Kevin has been in the interrogation room for over an hour."

Tears pooled in Abby's eyes. "He can't go to jail. Not because of me."

Jefferies smiled. "You're forgetting he's the son of a

Sinister Winds

cop. That boy lawyered up the second they put him in the room." Jefferies' smile disappeared. "You could learn a thing or two from your friend."

"I couldn't chance it. I was trying to protect my daughter. I figured the media would have been all over it, and whoever was out there would know where to find her." Abby fought back tears. "I've made a mess out of everything and don't know who to trust anymore. My parents weren't my parents. After Brian, I ran to Jacob. Then, I brought Kevin and his dad into all of this. I just can't seem to do anything right."

"It's hard to make good decisions when a puppet master is controlling your life." Jefferies sat back in his chair and intertwined his fingers. "Still, if you would have trusted me, I would have put you in a safe house."

"How did I know I could trust you?"

"To start, I'm with the FBI."

"Jacob told me he had friends in high places." Abby sniffed. "He had a judge in his pocket, for Pete's sake. I'd trusted Jacob all my life, and we see how well that turned out. I wanted to trust you. Especially since you said Eva sent you, but at the end of the day, I had my child to think of. I wasn't willing to place her life in the hands of a man I'd only known for a matter of minutes. For all I knew, someone could have told you about the dreams, and you were using me for information. If Eva is still visiting you, it's obvious she knows my baby is still in danger," Abby said, trying to control the panic that was building.

"Are you sure you can trust Mr. Bishop?" Jefferies asked.

"Kevin? Of course."

"What's his birthday?"

Abby shrugged. "I don't know."

"Where did he go to school? Did he attend college? What's his favorite color? What kind of music does he like? Do you see where I am heading with these questions?"

"Pink is his favorite color, as for all the rest, I don't know," Abby admitted.

"Is it possible that he's a plant?"

"No."

"Come on, Abby, look at all your husband has done up until this point. Don't you think he could put someone in place in a worst-case scenario? Someone who could continue to manipulate you."

"No…No, I don't believe it. I won't believe it! Kevin doesn't have a manipulative bone in his body."

"Just the same, I have asked Belinda to have a go at him. If he doesn't pass the smell test, then I'm going to have to ask you to trust me and sever all ties with the man."

"You mean not tell him I'm going to a safe house? I can't do that to him. He just lost his father. He'll be devastated."

"You're not going to a safe house," Jefferies said firmly.

"But Eva said…"

Jefferies softened his tone. "I'm offering you and your daughter something more permanent."

"I don't understand."

"We will place you into witness relocation, change your name, and find you a place to live where no one knows who you are. You will be given a new name, a place to live and we'll help you integrate into the community. You'll be able to put your baby into a stroller and take her for walks without fear. I'll monitor you myself," Jefferies promised.

Sinister Winds

Abby felt a glimmer of hope. "You really can do that?"

Jefferies smiled. "It's what I do. I've been giving it a lot of thought, and I think that's why Eva picked me. Somehow, she knew I would be able to help you."

"When?"

"It'll take a couple of days to set things up. We'll put you in a hotel under protective custody until we decide where we'll send you."

"Do I get a say?"

"Not usually. Where would you want to go?"

"I don't know. I was born in California. Maybe there." Abby had to admit Eva reaching out to Mr. Jefferies because she knew he could help made more sense than anything she'd thought of. "Do you think Kevin will go for it?"

Jefferies frowned. "You're not getting the point. No one can know you are there."

"You mean even if you clear him, Kevin won't be able to come with me?"

Jefferies shook his head. "I'm afraid not. That's the point of severing all ties."

Abby felt the shock of his words. "What?"

"That includes Mr. Bishop too. All of your friends, including Mr. Bishop. You'll not be able to go see him or call him. Ever," Jefferies said firmly.

Abby rose from her seat. "Not Kevin! He's my only friend. He doesn't have anyone else but me, and I promised his dad I would look after him."

Jefferies placed a hand on Abby's shoulder. "I'm sorry, but it can't be helped. If Nathan Riggs found you through Mr. Bishop, then anyone can. One phone call to the man would be all it would take for this whole thing to unravel. I'm sorry, Abby, but you're going to have to make a choice. It is the only way to keep you safe."

"But it was Edward's dying wish."

"I'm sorry, Abby," Jefferies repeated, standing firm.

Abby felt as if her heart would break. Kevin was the only friend she had left, and now, because of her, he would be all alone in the world. He had no family, no friends, and now she was getting ready to abandon him. It wasn't fair. Jefferies said she had a choice, but there wasn't one. If she stayed, she would be ensuring her baby would someday be taken from her. In the process, she or Kevin, maybe both, would likely be killed. Jefferies was right; she had to sever her relationship with Kevin. It was the only way to keep them all safe. Tears rolled down her face as she firmed her decision. "Okay, I'll do it. Can I at least tell Kevin goodbye?"

"No." Jefferies' forehead creased. "I'm sorry. It is just too risky. If he knows, then whoever comes looking for you will find a way to get him to talk or kill him for protecting you. I know it hurts, but I need you to trust me."

Abby brushed at the tears that continued to fall. "I am not doing this for me. I'm doing this to protect my baby and to protect Kevin. He's the only family I have left."

Jefferies brows went up in question.

"He's like a brother to me," Abby clarified. "You asked what I know about him. I know he's an orphan because of me, and he will likely be killed someday just because he knows me. You said it yourself; Kevin is already on their radar."

"I'll get a team to take you to the hotel," Jefferies said, turning on his heels and leaving without another word.

CHAPTER TWENTY

Abby wasn't sure what she expected when agreeing to the WITSEC program, but so far, the lack of security had her questioning if Mr. Jefferies would actually be able to protect her and her baby. Not only was she currently sitting in the last row of a plane headed to San Diego, but in the three days leading up to getting on the plane, she'd been able to go shopping for maternity clothes, take walks on the beach, and have dinners in the hotel restaurant. While she'd expected cloak and dagger, the only restrictions she found thus far were not being allowed to use the phone, speak to Kevin, or leave her hotel room unless supervised by her new babysitters, Agent Racheal Smith and Agent David Barnes. While she knew she should feel excited about the adventure to come, she only felt sorrow. Even though Kevin hadn't died, she mourned his loss all the same.

The captain came over the intercom, telling them of their imminent arrival to San Diego. Abby stared out the window, watching as the city came into view, and felt a wave of panic building.

Agent Belinda Winters, who'd joined Abby and the two agents on the flight, leaned in close and kept her voice low.

"Ready to start your new life?"

Abby continued to stare out the window. "A person could get lost down there."

"That's the plan," Winters replied. "Hand me your purse."

Abby pulled her attention from the window. "Excuse me?"

"Hand me your purse," the woman repeated.

Abby reached under the seat and pulled her bag free. The bag looked much different now that she'd turned over the money to Mr. Jefferies, who promised to set her up with a bank account and credit cards under her new name, which they'd yet to reveal.

"Bet you don't miss lugging around that heavy thing," Belinda said, handing the bag off to Agent Barnes in the seat across the aisle.

"I rather miss the weight of it," Abby said, watching as Agent Barnes handed it off to Agent Smith, who in turn gifted it to an older woman who had been wheeled onto the plane when the airport attendants asked for anyone needing assistance in loading the aircraft. While the woman had appeared frail at the time they wheeled her on board, she now looked full of life as she took the bag and handed them another.

Barnes handed the bag across the aisle. Belinda opened it, pulled out a wallet, and passed it to Abby.

Abby looked inside and blinked, surprised to see a photo of herself on a driver's license bearing the name Katherine Loraine Stephens. She frowned. Not really a name she would have chosen, but then again, it was tons better than Clennie Cloyce.

Belinda laughed. "You don't like it?"

"Do I have a choice?"

Sinister Winds

"Probably not at this point. The agency normally gives you names to correspond with your current initials, but Mr. Jefferies decided that wasn't the best course of action, since you were already found once."

"It's okay, I've heard worse. So I don't have to change my appearance?"

"No. It would be pretty hard to maintain a different look for a lifetime."

Abby swallowed. "A lifetime."

Belinda patted her on the arm. "It's going to be okay, Kattie."

"Kattie." Abby blew out a breath to calm herself as the wheels of the plane touched the runway.

"Okay, things are going to go fast from here on out. I want you to do whatever I tell you to do without stopping to ask questions. Got it?"

Abby nodded.

"Okay, here we go." Belinda turned to Barnes and gave a thumbs-up. To Abby's surprise, Belinda unbuckled, motioned Abby closer, then lifted her hair, twisting it on top of her head. "Hold it there."

Abby lifted a hand to her head, frowning when Belinda reached into her pocket and withdrew a scalp cover, which she tugged over Abby's head.

Belinda surveyed her work, tucking a strand here and there until she was satisfied. She reached out to Barnes, who handed her a messy grey wig, which she placed over the covering. She reached out her hand once more and Barnes gifted her with a pale yellow sweater. Belinda pointed to Abby's zippered sweatshirt. "Take that off and put this on," she said, handing her the sweater.

As soon as she did, Belinda stood and motioned her from the seat, handing her a pair of grass-colored polyester slacks. "Step behind that curtain and put these on."

Abby held them against the yellow sweater. "You're kidding, right?"

Reaching to unclamp her own hair, Belinda leveled a look at her.

"Fine. What about my dress?" she asked, stepping behind the curtain.

"Tuck it into the pants," Belinda replied.

Abby did as told, frowning at the bulky lumps beneath the pants. She did her best to smooth out the lumps then pulled the curtain aside and stared into the face of her clone.

With her hair brushed and lying against her shoulders, the woman now wore Abby's zippered hoody and an identical dress to the one Abby had on under the borrowed clothes. The woman smiled and turned so that Abby could see her protruding stomach. Abby gasped and stifled a giggle at seeing Belinda's hair sticking out in all directions.

Ignoring Abby's shock, Belinda snapped her fingers and demanded Abby's sandals.

Abby held on to the seat, took them off, and resisted a groan when Belinda handed her the woman's bright white sneakers in return.

"Go, the plane's nearly empty," Belinda said, then pulled a cloth from her bag and used it to remove her makeup.

The redhead slipped into the sandals, grabbed Abby's discarded purse, and headed up the aisle, with Agents Barnes and Smith following closely behind.

So much for there not being any cloak-and-dagger stuff.

"Sit and put on those shoes," Belinda said, pointing to the seat the body double had vacated.

Sinister Winds

Abby pulled on the shoes as Belinda shrugged into an oversized brilliant red sweater and matching hat. While a simple disguise, the woman was totally transformed.

"Come on, dear," Belinda said loudly. She reached out a hand to help Abby from the chair and leaned close, lowering her voice to a whisper. "Remember, you're old and feeble. Hunch over and take your time. Just before you get to the end, I want you to clutch your chest and claim to have trouble breathing."

Abby giggled nervously. "Maybe we should have rehearsed this?"

"Nonsense, you'll be fine. Just remember to keep that stomach covered."

To Abby's credit, she managed quite the performance, though she wavered briefly when a small airport emergency shuttle met them at the gate.

"It's all part of the plan. They're with us," Belinda said. "Just keep your head down and your stomach covered."

The shuttle raced them to the front of the building, where she and Belinda were loaded into a waiting ambulance, which left with the siren blaring.

"Take off those clothes," Belinda said, removing her hat and sweater. The ambulance swerved. Belinda beat on the side of the vehicle. "Hey, are you trying to kill us or what?"

"You want to drive?"

"No, just take it easy and kill that siren. You're giving me a headache, and unless you're a real paramedic, you don't want to have to deliver this baby," she yelled.

Abby stripped out of the pants and sweater and reached for the wig. "This too?"

"Unless you want to keep it for a souvenir," Belinda replied.

"Yeah, I think I'll pass," Abby said, pulling the wig and cap from her head. "Do you always work this way?"

Belinda smiled. "What? You don't like playing dress-up?"

"It's been a while," Abby said.

"Yeah, well, you better get used to it. We aren't done yet." She handed Abby a dress bag. "Put this on."

Abby unzipped the bag and pulled out a suit coat that looked two sizes too big. "Um, we might have a slight problem," she said, holding up the suit.

Belinda took the jacket. "That one's mine. Yours is on the other hanger."

Abby reached into the bag once more and brought out what looked to be a light pink jogging suit. Upon further inspection, she found it to be a pair of maternity overalls she'd eyed in the mall but decided they would be way too warm for California. "They are cute, but I'll probably suffocate."

"It gets cold on the plane," Belinda said as she worked to smooth her hair.

"The plane? I thought I was going to California."

"You did. You're just not staying here."

"Why not?"

"Because it's where you asked to go. The agency figures that if you want to go there, you've probably mentioned it to someone else along the way. So, your first choice is nearly always off the table."

"My first choice was my only choice," Abby said as she struggled to push her foot through the leg of the jumpsuit while balancing in the moving ambulance. "You know, I'm pretty sure this is against the law."

Belinda raised an eyebrow. "You want to file a grievance with the government, you can let Jefferies know when you see him."

"He's going to be on the plane?" Abby asked.

"We should be seeing him any minute," Belinda replied.

"Two minutes to the checkpoint," the driver called. "Be ready to jump and run."

Belinda smiled. "See, what did I tell you?"

Abby finished pulling the jumpsuit up and looked at Belinda. "Please tell me he doesn't mean that literally."

"He'll slow enough so you can tuck and roll," she said and winked.

The ambulance pulled into a parking garage, went up three levels, and stopped. A moment later, the door to the back opened.

Alfred Jefferies reached a hand in to help her down. "Mrs. Stephens, how was your flight?"

"Interesting," Abby replied.

Jefferies nodded to a black SUV with dark-tinted windows. "Your chariot awaits."

Abby stepped out of the ambulance and into a state of confusion. "Wait, are we at the airport?"

"I can't think of a better place to catch a flight," Jefferies said, opening the door to the SUV.

"But the lights and sirens?"

"All smoke and mirrors. They drove around until they made sure they weren't being followed, then met us back here." Jefferies shut the door then walked around and got in beside her as Belinda took the front passenger seat. As soon as the door shut, the SUV took off. Jefferies looked over at her. "I'm sure you have questions."

"Who was the woman who looked like me?"

"Abigail Buckley. At least for the time being. She'll go to your parent's grave and take up an apartment near your childhood home until after the baby is born. Unfortunately, there will be complications, and the child will not survive. After a brief time, Mrs. Buckley will take her own life and be mourned in a small ceremony and laid to rest next to her parents. Don't look so distressed, Mrs. Stephens. It's all smoke and mirrors. Libby is not actually pregnant. It is just another layer in place to keep you and your daughter safe."

"Where are we going?" Abby asked when the SUV exited the garage.

"Why, to the airport, of course," Jefferies replied.

Sure enough, the SUV pulled into a restricted drive and then continued onto the tarmac, coming to a stop in a hangar bay next to a Learjet. Abby looked over at Mr. Jefferies. "Is this your plane?"

"It belongs to the agency." The man smiled. "Care for a lift?"

"Where are we going?"

"Does it matter?"

Abby sighed. "I'm not sure anything matters anymore."

"Cheer up, Katherine. I think you're going to enjoy the next leg of the trip."

Doubtful, but she had to give it to the man. He'd held up his end of the bargain. "Mr. Jefferies, will I ever get used to my new name?"

"Yes, but it'll take time." He walked to the plane and motioned her to go first.

"I guess I have plenty of that," she replied. She started up the stairs and stopped. "What about my suitcase?"

"The ones you checked through belonged to Abby," he said with a grin. "Yours are already on the jet. I promise everything will be all right," he said when she hesitated once more.

"I'm not sure I can do this," she said, suddenly afraid.

216

"I want everything to be all right, but now it feels like it's all just another lie."

"Then remember why you are doing this and make it your truth." Jefferies glanced at her stomach. "The way up is the way out."

A chill raced up her spine as she realized the truth in Pearl's words.

A second SUV pulled up. The door opened. "ABBIEEEE!"

"Kevin?"

Kevin waved and hoisted a cat carrier for her to see, and suddenly, her new world felt a tad less empty.

"Your argument had merit." Jefferies grinned as he stepped aside. "Besides, the boy is so good at computers that it was only a matter of time before he found you."

EPILOGUE: A NEW BEGINNING

Abby pulled the wool scarf up to shield her face. "Holy smoke, can it get any colder?"

Kevin let out a snort. "We live in Michigan, and it is April. I assure you, this is not cold."

She pulled the zipper up higher on her coat. "I think we may be in trouble."

Kevin rolled his eyes. "Whose idea was it to move to Michigan?"

"You said you love Detroit. It sounded like a good idea at the time," Abby reminded him.

"Sunshine, we are nowhere near Detroit. We are in the frozen tundra. Just look at the map. Even Mother Nature saw the need to wrap most of the state in a glove to help keep it warm. We actually live in a mitten."

She looked around in a panic. "Don't say that!"

He tilted his head. "What? Mitten?"

"No, you can't use my old name, remember?"

"I didn't call you Abby. I called you Sunshine. Besides, Katherine is so... boring." He pursed his lips together in thought. "I know, I'll call you Kitten."

She smiled. "Don't you think that is a bit fresh, considering you're supposed to be my brother?"

"Pussy would be fresh; Kitten is fine," he assured her.

She relaxed. He was right; besides, anyone who spent time with Kevin for more than a few moments would realize he was not being fresh, not with her anyway. She veered the stroller around a puddle. "So, Tom," she said, using his new name. "Any regrets?"

"Sun...Kitten," he corrected, "before I met you, I was all alone in a town where I was considered normal. Now, I have something I never thought I would have. I have a family. I have a beautiful sister and an adorable niece, neither of which I would trade for anything in the world."

She glanced sideways at him. "It's not every day a girl can pick her own brother."

He snorted. "You make me sound like a puppy you picked up at the pound."

She sniffed in response.

"Don't you dare start crying," he warned. "Your tears will freeze to your face."

"I'm not crying. The cold is getting to me." They both remained quiet as two ladies approached. Wearing shorts and sweatshirts, the women both smiled and nodded their hellos. One of the ladies veered too close to the stroller, and the pup barked a sharp warning. Abby smiled at the little Doberman pup that was no taller than the stroller but made no move to correct him. He might just be a puppy, but he was to be the baby's bodyguard and was already showing great promise.

The lady smiled and backed away. "It's okay, big guy. I am not going to hurt your baby," she said, addressing the dog.

The woman turned her attention to Abby. "Dobermans are such wonderful dogs. My aunt used to have one. It saved the whole family from a house fire and wouldn't let anyone near my little cousin unless my aunt said it was okay."

Abby felt chills run along her spine. She had been worried about getting the dog, but all her research assured her this would be the best dog and one that would take his job seriously without any extra training beyond basic obedience. She had seen that firsthand with Killer, and that experience inspired her to research the breed.

Kevin had insisted upon naming the pup Preacher, saying that anyone who messed with either the dog or the baby would be praying by the time he was done with them.

The baby started whimpering.

"She might be too warm," the woman said, eying the snowsuit.

Abby's gaze drifted to the woman's bare legs. "We are not used to the cold."

Abby watched as the woman took in her attire. "Yes, I kind of gathered that. Are you just visiting, then?"

"No, we live here now."

"Oh? What brought you to our town?"

Kevin, who had been quiet until this time, jumped at this opening. "Witness relocation program."

Abby felt the color drain from her face. "Tom, what did Mr. Jefferies tell you about telling stories?" She turned back to the woman. "My brother has quite the imagination. I'm afraid it is nothing that romantic. We were just tired of city life. My brother's therapist thought the change would be good for him."

"I can understand change, but why Michigan? Why not pick someplace warm?" the woman said dreamily.

Abby was getting a bit put off by all the questions. What? Was the woman writing a book?

"We merely opened the atlas and picked a spot," she

said rather curtly.

The woman took the hint. "I'm sorry, you have to excuse all the questions. We don't get a lot of strangers around here. We are all pretty nosey, but I assure you we're harmless. I think you should stick to your brother's witness relocation story. Half the town will think you are being rude and won't want to talk to you, and the other half will think you are serious and realize you can't answer questions. Either way, it should stop those of us who can't help but ask a million questions."

Abby felt herself relaxing. After seeing how big San Diego was, she'd asked to be placed in a small town for just this reason. Outsiders didn't go unnoticed. On the off chance that anyone did find her and came poking around, she was fairly certain word would get back to her in time to do something about it.

The baby's whimper turned into a full cry. Abby picked her up to comfort her. Preacher sat, keeping his eyes trained on the child. As she bounced the baby, she noticed that the child was indeed sweating. Taking another look at the lady, she decided to remove the snowsuit. As she tugged at the sleeve, her daughter's top dropped down, exposing the birthmark just above her heart.

"A tattoo?" The second woman sounded surprised.

"A birthmark," Abby corrected, not bothering to tell the woman of its significance. Pearl had told her the child would be protected when she was born. Abby knew this to be true the moment she saw her daughter had a permanent chicken's foot to carry with her throughout her life.

"It looks like a talon," the woman mused.

"It's a chicken's foot," Kevin said, shaking his head. "Katherine here craved Kentucky Fried Chicken throughout her entire pregnancy."

This brought a chuckle from the woman. "Would you look at all that red hair. You sure can tell she is your daughter. What's her name?"

"Eva Pearl," Abby said with pride.

"What a beautiful name."

"Yes, it is a family name. She is named after her grandmother," Abby said, using the story they had composed.

"Your grandma must be very pleased," the woman said, waving at the baby.

"I hope so," Abby said. "She passed away a couple of years ago, but I like to think she is watching over her from heaven."

"I'm sure she is. We should all be so lucky to have a guardian angel."

"Your baby is well protected," the second woman mused.

The comment brought Abby up short. "Excuse me?"

"Yes, a grandmother looking down from heaven and a fearless protector here on earth, she said, nodding at Preacher. "Most pups that age would have been off seeing what they could sniff, but not that guy. He has not taken his eyes off of us. I think it is safe to say that no harm will ever come to her."

"I pray for that every single night," Abby said with a glance toward Kevin. "I guess it is all any mother ever wants for her child: a safe and happy childhood. I know that's what my mother wanted for me," Abby said, hugging her daughter close.

"Well, we're going to get going; we've taken up so much of your time. I'm sure this feels like an inquisition."

Abby cringed, remembering the real inquisition she'd endured months ago. "No, not at all," she said, meaning it.

Sinister Winds

The woman smiled. "I'm sure we will see you around town. It was great talking to you."

Abby made sure the woman was out of earshot before turning her attention to Kevin. "Really, Tom? Witness relocation? Why not just tell her our real names and get it over with?"

She watched as Kevin broke out in a huge grin. "What's so amusing?"

"I was just thinking how happy I am to have met you. I have a sister and an adorable niece. My legal name is Tom, and I live in Michigan," he said with a smile.

His enthusism was contagious. Abby put the baby back in the stroller and wrapped a blanket loosely around her legs.

"I'm happy too," she admitted. "I have a brother I can count on in an emergency, a beautiful daughter, and neighbors who care enough to be nosey."

Kevin chuckled. "Normal people would consider that an invasion of privacy."

Abby laughed. "Kevin, there isn't anything normal about either one of us."

Kevin leaned in and bumped her with his shoulder. "You got that right, Kitten. And don't call me Kevin."

CONNECT TO SHERRY A. BURTON

Please find it in your heart to take a moment and go to Amazon to leave a review. Reviews are also welcomed at Barnes & Noble, Bookbub, and Goodreads as well.

Most importantly, please tell EVERYONE and share in the reading groups! As an indie author, word of mouth is the best publicity I can get.

Thank you for taking this journey with me.

Sherry A. Burton

Please remember to follow me on Amazon and sign up for my newsletter on my website to keep up to date with all new releases.

Please sign up for my monthly author newsletter to keep up to date with all my random thoughts and book updates:
https://www.sherryaburton.com/

To order autographed copies of Sherry's books, go to www.dorrypress.com

Follow Sherry on social media:
https://www.facebook.com/SherryABurtonauthor
https://www.amazon.com/Sherry-A.-Burton/e/B005PM6QFG?ref=dbs_m_mng_rwt_auth
https://www.bookbub.com/profile/sherry-a-burton
https://www.instagram.com/authorsherryaburton

ABOUT THE AUTHOR

Sherry A. Burton writes in multiple genres and has won numerous awards for her books. Sherry's awards include the coveted Charles Loring Brace Award, for historical accuracy within her historical fiction series, The Orphan Train Saga. Sherry is a member of the National Orphan Train Society, presents lectures on the history of the orphan trains, and is listed on the NOTC Speaker's Bureau as an approved speaker.

Originally from Kentucky, Sherry and her Retired Navy Husband now call Michigan home. Sherry enjoys traveling and spending time with her husband of more than forty years.

Made in the USA
Middletown, DE
21 August 2025